Praise for Book One in the Sasquatch and Aliens series,

ALIEN ENCOUNTER

"[This] authentic, zany splash of fourth-grade humor, perspective, and imagination . . . will captivate elementary readers." —*School Library Journal*

"Funny and sweet." —*The Horn Book*

"Big-hearted, fast-paced, and deadpan. . . . Harper's journal-like blending of short chapters with humorous titles, comedic drawings, and lists succeeds to great effect." —*Publishers Weekly*

Charise Mericle Harper

SASQUATCH AND ALIENS

BOOK TWO

SUPER SASQUATCH SHOWDOWN

SQUARE FISH

Christy Ottaviano Books

Henry Holt and Company · New York

SQUARE
FISH

An Imprint of Macmillan
175 Fifth Avenue
New York, NY 10010
mackids.com

SUPER SASQUATCH SHOWDOWN. Copyright © 2015 by Charise Mericle Harper.
All rights reserved. Printed in the United States of America by
R. R. Donnelley & Sons Company, Harrisonburg, Virginia.

Square Fish and the Square Fish logo are trademarks of Macmillan and
are used by Henry Holt and Company, LLC under license from Macmillan.

Our books may be purchased in bulk for promotional, educational, or business use. Please
contact your local bookseller or the Macmillan Corporate and Premium Sales Department
at (800) 221-7945 ext. 5442 or by e-mail at MacmillanSpecialMarkets@macmillan.com.

Library of Congress Cataloging-in-Publication Data
Harper, Charise Mericle.
Super Sasquatch showdown / Charise Mericle Harper.
pages   cm. — (Sasquatch and aliens ; book 2)
"Christy Ottaviano Books."
Summary: "When Morgan and Lewis receive a cryptic letter and a key from Mr. Lee, they get to
see more of his lifelike costume creations. Robots, aliens, and Sasquatches abound, and the big
question through it all is—what's real and what's pretending to be real?"—Provided by publisher.
ISBN 978-1-250-11216-3 (paperback)   ISBN 978-1-62779-469-5 (ebook)
[1. Friendship—Fiction. 2. Extraterrestrial beings—Fiction. 3. Yeti—Fiction.
4. Northwest, Pacific—Fiction. 5. Humorous stories.] I. Title.
PZ7.H231323Str 2015   [Fic]—dc23   2014029988

Originally published in the United States by
Christy Ottaviano Books/Henry Holt and Company, LLC
First Square Fish Edition: 2016
Book designed by April Ward
Square Fish logo designed by Filomena Tuosto

1 3 5 7 9 10 8 6 4 2

AR: 4.1

For Vic and Lynn Doucet:
Thank you for the Sasquatch inspiration,
way back when I was only ten.
—xo Charise

Things I Normally Take to School

1) My backpack and my books.

What I Was Taking Today

1) My backpack and my books.
2) A chart that showed the things I knew about Mr. Lee.
3) A one-paragraph report about why plankton is important.

Sometimes when something is hard to explain, pictures and words work better than if you just used words all by themselves.

A lot of unusual things have happened since Lewis moved to town, and most of them have to do with Mr. Lee. Here's how those things happened.

① LEWIS AND I MEET BECAUSE OF UNDERPANTS IN A TREE. IT'S TRUE!

② LEWIS AND I BECOME FRIENDS. HEY!

③ LEWIS IS UNUSUAL.
-HE LIVES IN A MOTEL.
-HE CALLS HIS PARENTS BY THEIR FIRST NAMES. HI, SAGE! HI, DAVE!

④ LEWIS AND I SEE AN ALIEN IN THE WOODS.

⑤ WE TELL THE POLICE ABOUT THE ALIEN. OFFICER GARY DOES NOT BELIEVE US.

IT'S BALONEY!

⑥ MY NEIGHBOR MR. LEE SENDS US A NOTE TO COME MEET HIM.

⑦ MR. LEE TAKES US TO HIS SECRET STUDIO UNDER HIS GARAGE.

← THE ALIEN IS THERE.

⑧ MR. LEE SAYS THE ALIEN IS A ROBOT. MR. LEE MAKES SCARY ROBOTS FOR MOVIES.

MR. LEE →

I AM FAMOUS.

⑨ AS A FAVOR TO MR. LEE, OUR ALIEN SIGHTING CHANGES INTO A SASQUATCH SIGHTING.

⑩ MR. LEE PROMISES TO MAKE US COOL COSTUMES FOR HALLOWEEN.

⑪ LEWIS PICKS A DRAGON COSTUME. I STILL HAVEN'T PICKED ONE YET.

⑫ BECAUSE OF THE SASQUATCH SIGHTING, LEWIS'S MOTEL GETS LOTS OF GUESTS.

NO VACANCY

My Report About Plankton

Plankton are tiny living creatures that live in the sea. There are two kinds of plankton: phytoplankton, which are plants, and zooplankton, which are animals.

Phytoplankton are really important *because* they help make oxygen, and without oxygen people would die. Half of all the oxygen on Earth is made from phytoplankton. Zooplankton eats phytoplankton, and fish and whales eat zooplankton. Phytoplankton is the start of the food chain. If there were no plankton, Earth would *still be here* but all the people and animals would *probably be dead.* We should save plankton.

Why I Had to Write a One-Paragraph Report About Plankton

Mr. Lee asked me to write it. I have no idea why. Mr. Lee is not the kind of person you say no to, so I did it. I think it was a good paragraph. This is the letter he put in my mailbox.

Dear Morgan and Lewis,
When you come over on Friday, please bring a one-paragraph report on the importance of plankton. You each have to do your own.
Your friend,
Mr. Lee

I'm not quite sure if Mr. Lee is really our friend, but I guess he thinks he is. If a friend can be bossy, sneaky, and super mysterious, then Mr. Lee is that kind of friend.

What Is Hard and Not Fair

Going back to school on a Thursday after more than two weeks off! Thursday is only two days away from the weekend. Why couldn't we just start next Monday? I knew exactly who had thought of this—Mrs. Prigma, our principal. I wrote an acrostic about her, because sometimes that's just the fastest way to explain someone.

PROBABLY WORKS ON THE WEEKENDS

REALLY LIKES TO TORTURE KIDS

IS KIND OF SCARY TO STAND NEXT TO

GETS JOY OUT OF LONG, BORING SPEECHES

MAYBE EVEN DREAMS ABOUT SCHOOL

ALWAYS SAYS, "LEARNING COMES FIRST!"

I like acrostics. I make them up when I'm nervous, upset, or bored, and usually after making one, I feel better. But not today. When I finished "Prigma," I felt exactly the same as when I'd started it. Every part of my brain and body still wanted to stay home.

Mom could tell something was up, because normally she doesn't come outside and watch me walk to school, but today she did. She stood on the sidewalk and waved until I turned the corner. She was right to be worried, because what I really wanted to do was sneak back home and hide in the basement.

HOW TO GET INTO THE HOUSE
WITH NO ONE SEEING YOU

SNEAK AROUND TO THE SIDE OF THE HOUSE.

CLIMB IN THROUGH THE BROKEN BASEMENT WINDOW.

What I Should Have Been Excited About

1) Lewis was going to be in class with me at school—AWESOME!
2) Everyone was going to be freaking out that Lewis and I had seen a real, live Sasquatch.
3) Mrs. Shipley, my teacher, was probably going to be nicer to me because I'd been in the newspaper, and she loves the news.

But instead of being excited about any of that, I was thinking about Marcus Wolver. If people could be things, Marcus would be a giant dark cloud of rain that always showed up to ruin something fun that was about to happen.

OH NO! NOT A MARCUS WOLVER STORM CLOUD!

HE RUINS EVERYTHING!

PICNIC

I was glad when I ran into Carla Minkel a block later. She's not a good friend or anything, but she likes to talk, and listening to her was better than being in my brain with Marcus Wolver.

When she saw me, the first thing she said was, "Look, you got glasses."

I was going to hear a lot of that today. I thought of a funny comeback, but I didn't say it.

Carla is pretty serious about stuff, and she's not very good with jokes. Sometimes she kind of reminds me of my sister, Betty, but Carla's not as weird. Or as strong—there's no way she'd be able to hold me in a headlock.

Of course she'd heard about the alien/Sasquatch thing. I thought she'd ask all sorts of questions, but mostly she just wanted to know what kind of tortilla chips the Sasquatch had taken.

She said, "I don't want to be a Sasquatch magnet."

I didn't know how to answer her, so I just nodded like I was agreeing. She was grumpy that I couldn't remember the exact brand of the chips, but I did a good job of describing the package, so really she shouldn't have been complaining.

As soon as we got to the playground, we could tell something was going on. Normally kids are screaming and running all over, but today everyone was clumped together in a huge group in front of the slide. Was somebody hurt? Was it a fight? I left Carla and ran over to look.

The Surprise on the Slide

It wasn't a fight. It was Lewis, and everyone was crowded around listening to him! It was like he was famous or something. And then my mouth fell open, because standing right next to him, with a giant smile on his face, was Marcus Wolver. Were Lewis and Marcus friends? When had that happened? Today? I wanted to turn around and leave, but before I could move, Lewis spotted me.

No way! I was not going up there.
I shook my head and took a few steps back.

Some people might think it's fun to stand on top of a slide in front of thirty people, but I'm not one of those people. I'm more of an I'm-OK-here-near-the-back-of-the-crowd-as-long-as-I-have-a-good-view kind of person. I don't know why, but there's something different between standing in front of thirty people at the playground and standing in front of thirty people in the classroom. The classroom isn't as scary.

I moved backwards—mostly for safety, because Lewis doesn't always understand head shaking, and sometimes he doesn't even understand the word *no*. It was easy to imagine him charging down, grabbing my arm, and dragging me up the slide, but luckily that didn't have a chance to happen because two seconds later the bell rang.

Lewis patted Marcus on the shoulder, waved at me to wait, and slid down the slide. I was worried that Marcus was coming too, but he just stood there looking down at us, slowly losing his smile until he looked the same as he always did—scowling and grumpy.

What I Had to Ask

"How come you're hanging out with Marcus Wolver?"

Lewis punched me in the arm and grinned.

"Why? Are you jealous?"

Instantly my face was hot. I knew why. I was blushing! Really? This had to happen now? I looked at the ground and hoped that Lewis hadn't noticed. The blushing was all Mom's fault.

WE COME FROM A LONG LINE OF BLUSHERS.

MOM SMILING LIKE WE SHOULD BE PROUD OF THIS.

MOM BLUSHING WHILE SHE IS TALKING.

"Just kidding!" said Lewis, and he punched me again. "Marcus is part of the plan."

I nodded like I knew what he was talking about, but I didn't have a clue. Lewis is the king of plans. He's always thinking of something new, but why include Marcus Wolver? Lewis followed me up the steps and into school. Three minutes later we were outside Room 401, Mrs. Shipley's class.

Lewis was excited. This was his big day—new school, new class, new teacher, new kids—and anything could happen. I didn't want to ruin it for him, but he was wrong about the "anything could happen" part. Once he got his new books and his new desk, the fun would be over. Nothing exciting ever happened in Room 401.

What Was Not Good

My face was still red. I could feel it.

You'd think that a family of blushers would have come up with some way to control unwanted blushing, but Mom said there was no cure. No medicine. No tricks. No nothing. You just had to wait for it to go away. I kept my head down. Hiding it was all I could do.

Suddenly two giant feet were in front of me, then a hand grabbed my shoulder—Mrs. Shipley!

"Well, well, what have we here? Chin up."

When I looked at her, she scrunched her nose and snorted, then patted my shoulder.

"No need to be embarrassed. I'll be expecting your full attention now that you can see." Then she winked and touched her own glasses. "Welcome to the club."

It was instant embarrassment plus! I could feel my face turn even redder. In a club with Mrs. Shipley? Not good news! Hopefully no one had heard her. I left Lewis at the door and escaped to my desk. He didn't need me. Lewis could take care of himself.

As soon as I sat down, I made up an acrostic.

SOMETIMES MAKES ME NERVOUS

HAS EYES IN THE BACK OF HER HEAD

IS GOOD AT CATCHING ANYONE FOOLING AROUND

PROBABLY LOVES GRADING TESTS

LETS PEOPLE GO TO THE BATHROOM WHEN THEY ASK

EVEN GIVES TESTS ON FRIDAY AFTERNOONS

YELLS WHEN SHE IS REALLY MAD

It helped, but only for a little bit.

What I Was Right About

After Lewis was introduced, got his books, and
sat down, nothing else fun happened for the rest
of the morning. It was a relief when the bell rang
for lunch. Lewis was waiting for me in the hall.
He looked disappointed.

"This school isn't as fun as my old school," he said.

I nodded. "I know. I told you so."

Lunch

By the time we got to the lunchroom, Lewis
was over being upset. He was excited again, this
time about the cafeteria. Friends shouldn't let
friends eat UFL—Unidentified Food Lumps—so
I warned him.

I pointed to the lunch display. "Look, it's
probably not even real food. You can have half of
my lunch from home."

Lewis put his hand up. "Thanks, but no thanks.
I'm sick of real food. I need a break from seeds,
nuts, and vegetables. Do you know how hard it
was to get Sage to let me eat at school?"

I shook my head.

Lewis was quiet for a few seconds, then added, "Well, it was really hard."

Lewis's mom is a health nut. If she knew what he was about to eat, she'd flip out. Lewis picked up a tray and marched toward the food line. It wasn't long, because every day more and more kids brought their lunches from home. I followed Lewis, but only to watch.

Lewis pointed to the lumpy mounds, and the lunch ladies piled them onto his plate. He even asked for some of a greenish mound. I wasn't the only one surprised by that.

HOW THE LUNCH LADY LOOKS
IF YOU ASK FOR THE GREEN STUFF

What Was a Surprise
to Everyone at Our Table

Lewis ate every single thing on his plate.

All of it! Even the green stuff! And after the

last bite, he said, "Do you think I can get more of that green one?"

Nobody answered. We were all too shocked and disgusted.

After we were done eating, the number one thing everyone wanted to talk about was us seeing the Sasquatch. Lewis and I took turns telling the story, but he was a lot better at it than me. At the Lewis parts, everyone laughed, but when I told my parts, people just smiled.

KID LISTENING TO LEWIS

← LAUGHING SO HARD ORANGE JUICE SQUIRTED OUT OF HIS NOSE

Marcus Wolver was sitting two tables away with his usual gang. Some of those kids like Lee and Trevor are actually kind of nice, so it's a mystery why they like him. I was glad that Lewis's plan didn't include Marcus sitting with us.

Watching Lewis eat school food was hard

enough. Adding Marcus Wolver to the mix would have totally killed my appetite.

After lunch, Lewis and I went outside to discuss his plan. A few kids followed us out, but Lewis told them we had to be private to talk about secret Sasquatch business. I was a little surprised that no one laughed at that.

We walked all the way to the school fence, so no one could hear us.

As soon as we got there, Lewis said, "OK, let's see the note."

I pulled out both notes and held them up. "Which one?" I asked. Lewis pointed, and I put the plankton note back in my pocket. Even though we'd read them both about twenty times already, it was still exciting.

Dear Morgan and Lewis,
Please use the enclosed key to open my side garage door. Come at 2 p.m. on Friday. Do not let anyone follow you. I need to talk to you about my Sasquatch.
Your friend,
Mr. Lee

I pointed to the 2 p.m. part. "That won't work. School isn't over until three."

Lewis nodded. "It's OK. We'll just be a little late."

An hour seemed more than a little late, but I didn't argue. We could waste time on that later. Right now there were two things I needed to know. Why was Marcus Wolver in Lewis's plan? And had Lewis written his paragraph about plankton? But before I could ask anything, Lewis pointed to the note, put his finger on the word *my*, and nodded his head.

"Right there. That's the most interesting word in this whole note. Do you know why?"

I smiled. That was easy. A second later, Lewis said the exact words that I was thinking.

Before Lewis could start talking about anything else, I asked him about the plankton paragraph. Had he done it? He shook his head, then promised he'd have it for tomorrow. I hoped so. Mr. Lee was the kind of person who would say, "No plankton paragraph equals no Sasquatch robot." And I didn't want anything to go wrong.

Lewis's Big Plan

Let Marcus Wolver see the Sasquatch.

The plan was only six words long, but it filled my brain with questions.

"How? Why? Where? When?"

Instead of answering, Lewis just smiled. Now I was nervous.

I AM NOT DRESSING UP LIKE A SASQUATCH AGAIN!

I shook my head. "I'm not wearing that costume!"

Lewis nodded.

"You're right, no dressing up. This time it has to be the real thing."

Conversations with Lewis are not easy. He never answers questions in the order that you ask them.

"You're going to love this," said Lewis. "Guess who is Marcus's dad?"

Classic Lewis: answer a question with a question! I gave up. Fine, he could have it his way. But I wasn't going to make it easy. I pretended to be thinking hard and then said, "Darth Vader."

Lewis nodded. "Pretty close. He's evil and he wears a uniform, but he doesn't have a theme song."

I shrugged.

Lewis leaned in close. "It's Officer Gary, that mean police officer guy we met."

MY MIND BEING BLOWN

WHAT?!

HOLDING MY HEAD SO IT DOESN'T EXPLODE

"Officer *Gary* is Marcus's dad? Officer Gary is *Marcus's* dad?" I had to say it a couple of times to get my brain to believe it.

Lewis nodded. "I know. Perfect, right?"

Officer Gary was the police officer we'd met when we reported our alien sighting. You'd think he would've been interested in keeping the community safe, but no. He just thought we were wackos. He didn't make fun of us, but we'd left the police station knowing exactly what he thought of our story.

My brain matched them up side by side, Officer Gary and Marcus Wolver. Of course they were related. They had the same personality—grumpy and unlikable. Wait! What was Lewis talking about? What was perfect? I looked back at him.

Lewis was watching me like he was waiting for my brain to catch up. Lewis was smarter than me, I knew that, but still it was annoying. No one likes to be slow. It was probably all the seeds and nuts his mom made him eat, but still, I wasn't going to eat his mom's muffins. Nothing was worth that.

Why Lewis's Plan Was Perfect

There was one surprisingly good reason.

1) People believe police officers.

After we saw the Sasquatch, Lewis's parents' motel got a ton of customers. Everyone wanted to see the Sasquatch, but now it wasn't as busy anymore.

"We need to get more business," complained Lewis. He looked worried. Lewis never got worried. Something was up.

"We need another Sasquatch sighting," said Lewis. "Only this time it can't be us seeing the Sasquatch. That'd be too suspicious. But if Marcus saw the Sasquatch, that'd be perfect."

Lewis took a step back so he could wave his arms around without hitting me. Big ideas need arm movements.

Lewis put his hands up and continued. "If Marcus sees the Sasquatch, he'll tell his dad, and then his dad, Mr. Police Officer, will tell the world."

If Lewis were a villain, he would have thrown in an evil laugh like MWAHAHAHAHA. But he wasn't, so he just stood there and smiled.

"We just need to get Mr. Lee to march his Sasquatch around so Marcus can see it." Lewis took a deep breath. "It would solve everything, because if this motel business fails, we'll probably have to move away."

The Two Words That Surprised Me

Move away?

What was he talking about?

Lewis shook his head. "I know, but it's what we do. When things don't work out, we move, and right now the motel business is not awesome."

Lewis had never said anything about this before. How many times had he moved? Before I could ask the question, he answered it.

"We've moved twenty-five times since I was two."

I couldn't believe it. "But that's more than once a year! And you'd move again, so soon?"

Lewis shrugged. "I don't know. Maybe. Probably. But I don't want to, and neither does Red. So we have to do something. Something so we can stay."

What I Didn't Say

"You're the coolest friend I've ever had. I don't want you to move away!"

What I Did Say

"You're right. We have to do something!"

The One Giant, Impossible Problem with Lewis's Plan

Mr. Lee.

Just thinking about it made me shake my head. "Mr. Lee won't do it."

Lewis was the opposite of me. He was nodding. "He will if we find his weak spot. We have to find a way to make him say yes."

As we walked back toward the school, I had two more questions.

"Why was Marcus Wolver standing next to you, and why was he smiling?"

"I promised him something," said Lewis. He looked down at the ground and then mumbled the answer.

I couldn't believe it, but it made sense. Marcus was an expert rumor-ruiner. I don't know why people believed him, but they did.

What Lewis Didn't Want Marcus to Say

Lewis had stopped him before he could start. That was good thinking.

How I Knew Lewis Was Really Serious About Being Worried

If Lewis's worry about having to move was bigger than his love for his dragon costume, then this was serious, because up until today, the one thing Lewis loved more than anything else in the whole world was his dragon costume.

THE DRAGON COSTUME

SMOKE FROM HERE

SMOKE FROM HERE

When the bell rang for us to go back inside, Lewis and I still hadn't thought of a way to get Mr. Lee to help us. Walking back into school felt like marching toward doom. My feet were moving forward, but the rest of my body wasn't happy about it.

It didn't help that we knew what we'd be doing all afternoon: reading tests. Sometimes if you make fun of something you don't want to do, it can make you feel better about it, but I couldn't think of one single joke to make about having to do reading tests.

How I Feel About Reading Tests

I hate them. Mostly it's because of the bad stories. Who writes those things? *Sammy Loses a Tooth, A Beaver Makes a Home, Let's Help Dad Fix the Sink.* It's always the kind of thing you'd never read unless a teacher made you. Then there was the flipping the pages back and forth a million times to find the answers to the questions. The whole thing was one hundred percent NOT fun.

What Happened in the Afternoon That Was Interesting

Nothing.

I couldn't wait for the day to end. There's a clock on the wall behind me, but I could only look at it every couple of minutes because if Mrs. Shipley catches you turning around a lot, she gets mad.

WHAT MRS. SHIPLEY WOULD SAY

IF SHE CAUGHT ME

WHY SO INTERESTED IN THE CLOCK, MR. HENRY? DO YOU HAVE SOMEWHERE YOU'D RATHER BE? PLEASE TELL US ABOUT IT.

The minute the bell rang, I was out the door. Almost. A hand grabbed my shoulder and held me back. It was Mrs. Shipley.

"So, Mr. Henry, is it true? Did you really see it?"

For a second, I was confused. Was she asking about the clock or the Sasquatch? I nodded, hoping not to get in trouble. Then Mrs. Shipley surprised me. She leaned in close and whispered, "Me too. I saw the Sasquatch, but it was just a glimpse."

Suddenly I was in the hallway. Someone had pushed me from behind. When I looked back, Mrs. Shipley was talking to someone else.

Walking Home

Lewis and I walked out of the schoolyard together, but only as far as the main sidewalk. After that, we had to go in different directions—me toward town and Lewis toward the woods.

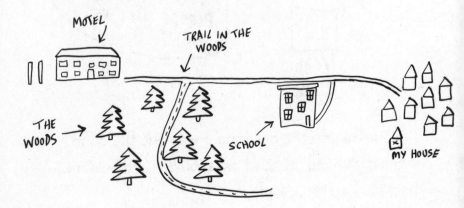

I pulled out my Mr. Lee chart and showed it to Lewis. Maybe there'd be a clue to get Mr. Lee to help us.

Chart About Mr. Lee

FACTS	TRUE	NOT TRUE	NOT SURE
Mr. Lee makes robot models for movies.	We have seen the robots.		He could be doing other things too.
Mr. Lee has a secret studio under his garage.	We have seen the secret studio.		
Mr. Lee has stuff written in a strange language in his studio.	Mr. Lee says it's a special language for movie designers.		
Mr. Lee is mysterious.	Mr. Lee does not like to use the phone. He sends us notes instead.		
Mr. Lee is famous.			He says he is, but we had never heard of him before.

We studied the chart for a few minutes but couldn't find any clues. Mostly it just made me think of more questions. *Why did Mr. Lee trust us? Why did his studio have to be a secret? Was he really a famous movie model maker? Why didn't he live in a big, fancy house? Why did he use notes to talk to us? Why did we have to write a paragraph about plankton?*

Too many questions can make a brain hurt, so I finally put the chart away. Neither of us had any answers.

Before we separated, we each promised to try to think of a plan for tomorrow, some way to get Mr. Lee to help. I smiled so Lewis would think I was excited and full of energy, but my true feelings were the opposite.

What I Did Not Need to See the Minute I Walked into My House

Betty dancing with a broom. And not just a regular broom but a broom with a paper bag on the end of it decorated like a head. It was embarrassing. She was lucky Lewis wasn't with me. But then, Lewis and Betty were kind of the same about embarrassment—it didn't bug them.

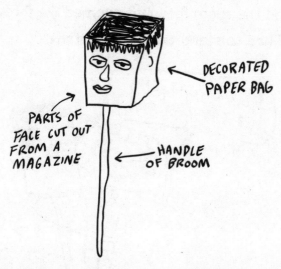

DECORATED PAPER BAG

PARTS OF FACE CUT OUT FROM A MAGAZINE

HANDLE OF BROOM

I slammed the door. I didn't mean to. It was an accident. Instantly Betty stopped dancing, turned to me, and scowled.

"Thank you very much! Now I'll have to start counting all over again."

I looked around the room. What was she counting? Wondering about it was a mistake. I should have ignored her, walked straight to the kitchen, and just gotten a snack, but I didn't. Instead I did something stupid—really stupid. I asked her a question.

"What are you counting?"

"Steps," said Betty. "Watch!"

And then she and the broom did bad dancing all around the room for what seemed like forever! And I had to stand there and watch it.

When she was finally done, she flopped onto the couch and dropped the broom.

She growled and gave it a kick. "Stupid broom. I need a real partner. Dancing with a stick is too hard."

I took a step back toward the door.

Betty saw me and laughed. "Eww, not you! I need a bigger partner. Someone tall, like Dylan." Betty sat up and pointed to a spot above her head. "He's taller than me." Then she flipped her hair around, like someone other than me was watching. It was good she was busy, because I was busy too—rolling my eyes. Betty is crazy. Here's proof.

Number One

Betty thinks that Dylan, an eighth grader, is going to pick her to be his dance partner for some kind of competition her school is having.

Number Two

Betty and her friends all have pretend boyfriends. Yup. Boyfriends who are one hundred percent imaginary—made up and NOT real. They say it's so they can practice for when they get real boyfriends. I'm not usually a squasher of dreams, but sometimes the fantasy just needs to end and the truth needs to be told.

Last week Betty's pretend boyfriend was named Jason, but this week she dumped him because now she's obsessed with Dylan. He's real, but he doesn't know she exists—so it's pretty much the same thing as before.

BETTY GIVING ME WAY TOO MUCH INFORMATION

What I Know

- Betty can't dance.
- *Dylan* is not a French name.
- Her life is not going to change.

WHAT DYLAN DOES NOT LOOK LIKE

How I Made My Escape

Sometimes you have to treat Betty like a wild animal: keep eye contact and move slowly, because if you look away she could attack, and she's got a mean headlock. I started backing out of the room one step at a time. Betty was still talking, now about how much she hated the broom. I nodded like I was agreeing with her, but mostly I wasn't listening.

Who Saved Me

Mom.

SINCE YOU HAVE THAT BROOM OUT, WHY DON'T YOU DO SOME SWEEPING?

I don't know why Mom giving Betty a chore was my fault, especially since Betty got the broom out in the first place, but Betty was glaring at me. She made a big show of pulling the bag head off the broom, and then she stomped all over it. I got out of there fast, while Mom was still around. I usually eat my snack in the kitchen, but today that was too dangerous. I grabbed a banana and headed straight to my room. You wouldn't think a sign on a door would work, but it does. Betty never comes in.

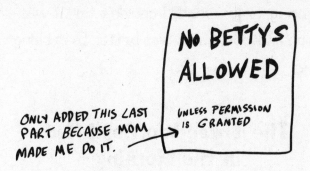

NO BETTYS ALLOWED

UNLESS PERMISSION IS GRANTED

ONLY ADDED THIS LAST PART BECAUSE MOM MADE ME DO IT.

What Happened at Dinner

Betty was still grumpy. Once she gets in a bad mood, she really likes to stay there.

BETTY'S QUALITIES THAT WILL NOT GET HER A BOYFRIEND

ARMS THAT CAN PUT YOU IN A HEADLOCK

MEAN LOOK ON FACE

MOUTH THAT TALKS ABOUT HERSELF ALL THE TIME!

I was glad when dinner was finally over, and extra glad that Betty spent the whole rest of the night stomping around in her room. Was she dancing, or just mad? I couldn't tell. It was annoying and loud, but it was better than being near her.

The Three Worries I Had in the Morning

1) I didn't have a good idea for getting Mr. Lee to help us.
2) We were going to be late to see Mr. Lee.
3) Lewis hadn't done his paragraph about plankton.

When I got to school, Lewis was waiting for me by the gate. I was glad we were both early—it gave us time to talk, and maybe even do something about worry number two.

I pointed down the street. "What if we go to Mr. Lee's house and leave him a note so he'll know we'll be late? If we run, I bet we can get back here before the bell rings."

Lewis shook his head and started walking toward the school. "Naw, it'll be fine. Where's he going to go? He'll just be working in his studio."

I nodded. Lewis was probably right. Mr. Lee was always making things. The one time we'd visited his studio, it had been crammed full of stuff he was working on.

Lewis's Big Worry

We still didn't have a good idea for getting Mr. Lee to help us.

"I thought you'd think of one," he said. "I was

pretty busy with the plankton paragraph." He pulled a crumpled paper ball out of his pocket, held it up, and then shoved it back in again. That should have made me feel better, but it didn't. It only made me wonder if Mr. Lee was going to be picky about neatness.

"Hey," said Lewis. "Did you know that plankton are two different things? Phytoplankton are plants and zooplankton are animals."

I nodded.

"And guess who eats the most zooplankton?"

That was an easy one, but I didn't answer. Maybe if he told me, it would cheer him up.

Lewis studied a rock by his foot and kicked it. I was waiting for him to say, "Blue whales," but instead he just said, "Aw, forget it. It won't matter anyway."

I nodded. It was hard to be excited about plankton when the real problem in your life couldn't be solved. Lewis and I just stood there, kicking stones until the bell rang. It was a bad way to start the day.

Mrs. Shipley was standing at the door when we walked in. She winked at me as I went by.

What Is Always a Fun Surprise

Days that get changed around because of teacher meetings.

↑ TEACHERS ↑

As soon as everyone was sitting down, Mrs. Shipley said, "I have to go to a teachers' conference this afternoon, so we won't be on our regular schedule."

"What are we going to do?" shouted Jack.

STUDENTS

Mrs. Shipley is usually strict about raising your hand for questions, but today she didn't seem to notice.

She grabbed a piece of paper off her desk, studied it, and then said, "Dodgeball."

Half the class groaned and half the class cheered. Dodgeball is like that. If you're on a good team it's fun, but if you're on a bad team it's the opposite of fun—totally painful!

After that, the rest of Friday morning was the same as it always was. While we were supposed to be working on math, I thought about a different team—Team Sasquatch. It was a very small team: me, Lewis, Dad, Red, Lewis's parents, and Mrs. Shipley—we were the Sasquatch believers. But if we got Marcus Wolver on our team, then we'd be bigger. Maybe even big enough that Lewis wouldn't move away. We just needed Mr. Lee!

WITHOUT MR. LEE

WITH MR. LEE

Fantasy Thinking

This seemed like a good idea only for about two seconds, because there's one very important thing about Mr. Lee that is impossible to ignore—Mr. Lee is not a helpful person. When we'd been in trouble before, after seeing the alien—even though it was *his* alien robot—he didn't help us, not one little bit. I spent all morning trying to come up with a plan, but when the lunch bell rang, I still had nothing.

Lunchtime

When we got to the cafeteria, Lewis picked up a tray and stood in line. It was hard to believe he really liked the food, but if you see something with your own eyes, you have to believe it. While I waited for him at the table, I made up an acrostic.

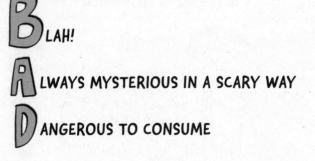

Blah!

Always mysterious in a scary way

Dangerous to consume

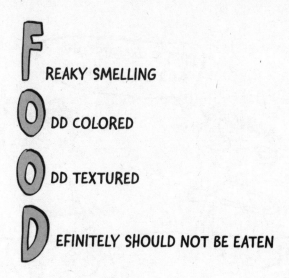

FREAKY SMELLING

ODD COLORED

ODD TEXTURED

DEFINITELY SHOULD NOT BE EATEN

"I got extra meatloaf," said Lewis, and he banged his tray down. "Do you want some?"

I studied his plate. It was loaded with blobs of brown, green, and tan. I didn't want any of it, but I was curious. "Which one's the meatloaf?"

Lewis studied his plate. He started to point to the biggest lump but then changed his mind.

He shrugged. "I forgot. I guess I'll have to taste it."

I waited, but after he was done tasting, he just shrugged again. He pointed to two different lumps of brown. "It's got to be one of these." Then he smiled and kept eating until everything was gone.

"Man, I love dodgeball!" said Lewis. He dropped his fork onto his empty tray, then sat dead still, not moving, like he was thinking about something.

I was thinking about something too. People don't love something unless they are good at it. No matter what, I needed to get on Marcus's team.

Lewis stood up, pointed to some streaks in the middle of his plate, and said, "I'm getting more of this one."

I didn't answer—I was too busy staring over his shoulder. It was Marcus Wolver, and he was heading right for us.

He stopped in front of Lewis. "You're a liar," snapped Marcus. "Everyone says it's impossible!" His face was red, like a volcano about to explode.

Surprise

Lewis hardly ever gets surprised, but Marcus had done it. Lewis dropped his tray. It clattered onto the table and then crashed to the floor. The fork, though, was saved. Lewis opened and closed his hand, like he was surprised to see it there. Everyone in the cafeteria was watching.

Marcus pointed at Lewis. "That dragon costume you promised me isn't real! I looked for it on the Internet and it doesn't exist. You tried to trick me! You made it up!" Marcus was wrong, but we couldn't tell him that. Mr. Lee was going to make the costume, but that was a secret—a secret we couldn't share. Marcus stopped talking and looked around to make sure he had an audience, then he smiled. Marcus Wolver smiling was not a good thing. He took a step toward Lewis. Now they were face-to-face.

Lewis's hand tightened around the fork until it was a fist. This wasn't good, but I couldn't do anything to help. My body was frozen.

Marcus poked Lewis in the chest. "YOU MADE IT UP! Just like you made up the Sasquatch story! And you did it all on purpose, to FOOL US!" Marcus took a step back and opened his arms, like the *us* he was talking about was everyone in the room, and they were all on his side. Then he said something even worse.

"Even my dad thinks so, and he's a police officer."

What Surprised Everyone

Lewis laughed. And it wasn't a little laugh like he was nervous—it was a huge laugh, as if what Marcus had said was the funniest thing he'd ever heard.

WHY IS HE LAUGHING?

ME WATCHING LEWIS

What Surprised Marcus

After a few seconds, everyone started talking again, and Lewis wasn't the center of attention anymore.

Lewis looked at Marcus, pointed to his tray on the floor, and said, "Do you want to pick that up, or should I?"

Marcus didn't answer. He just turned and walked off in a cloud of darkness.

MARCUS WALKING
AWAY

When Marcus was gone, I helped Lewis pick everything up. He wasn't smiling anymore. Instead he looked tired. It didn't matter. He was a hero. I'd never seen anything like that before.

I patted him on the back. "That was awesome. How did you know it would work?"

Lewis sighed. "I've had a lot of practice. Remember all the moving? That's sixteen new schools. By now, I've pretty much perfected that laugh."

I didn't know what to say.

Lewis shrugged. "It's OK," he said. He forced a smile. "I guess I got my costume back."

I tried to smile too, but my brain was thinking of something else—something that was hard to smile about.

What Was Lucky About Dodgeball

Whenever we play a team sport, Mr. Smithfield, the PE teacher, usually picks the captains and then lets them pick their own team, but today he didn't do that. He picked the whole teams himself. I was nervous. Would Lewis and Marcus be against each other? The only good thing was that we weren't playing dodgeball to the death.

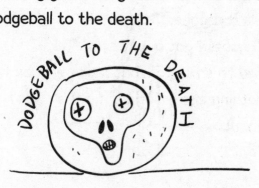

DODGEBALL TO THE DEATH

Mr. Smithfield must have known about the cafeteria trouble, because the first three people he picked for team one were Lewis, Marcus, and me. That was too big of a coincidence to be an accident. I was worried about being on the same team as Marcus now, but once we started the game, I was glad that we didn't have to play against him—he's really good! It must have made him crazy that he wasn't allowed to whip the ball at Lewis or me. Being on a good team made all the difference. When we were done, I said something to Lewis I had never said before.

I LIKE DODGEBALL!

After dodgeball there were still twenty minutes of school left. Mr. Smithfield sent us to the library to wait for the bell. Most people were looking at books or fighting over the three library iPads, but Lewis and I just sat on the chairs closest to the door and waited for the hands of the clock to reach twelve and three. It was slow torture.

What Lewis Asked Me More Than Five Times

"Are you sure you have the key?"

Each time he asked, I patted my pocket and said yes, but finally I just took it out and showed it to him. It was the first time I'd ever seen Lewis anxious, nervous, and worried all at the same time. But I didn't have to think very hard to figure out why.

As soon as the bell rang, we took off running. We only made one stop—our lockers. Twelve minutes later, we were standing in front of Mr. Lee's garage. I opened my backpack and got everything out. This wasn't going to be like last time. This time, we were going in prepared.

STICK FOR SAFETY

BACK PACK WITH CAMERA

KEY

DOUBLE SLINGSHOT IN CASE OF EMERGENCY

The Surprising Thing Lewis Asked Me

"Should I cry?"

"What?" Did he say *cry*? I looked at him. Was he sad? "Now?"

"No, later," said Lewis. "When we ask Mr. Lee about showing Marcus the Sasquatch. Do you think it would help? Because I can do it, just like I did the laughing thing."

"Really? Real tears and everything?"

Lewis nodded.

I fumbled in my pocket for the key while I thought about it. Crying was all we had. It wasn't great, but it was better than nothing.

I turned to Lewis. "Definitely, you should do it."

Who knew? Maybe we'd get lucky. Maybe Mr. Lee was one of those people who was a sucker for tears.

WHAT MR. LEE WOULD PROBABLY SAY

HERE'S A TISSUE. I DON'T CARE ABOUT YOUR CRYING.

We were already late, so I walked up to the garage door, put the key into the lock, and opened the door. Since this was our second visit to Mr. Lee's, I had an idea of what to expect. This time I was more excited than nervous. It was like riding a roller coaster—the second time is more fun.

FIRST TIME ON ROLLER COASTER

SECOND TIME ON ROLLER COASTER

What I Was Expecting

1) We'd open the door and it'd be dark inside.
2) Mr. Lee would suddenly turn on the lights.
3) We'd follow Mr. Lee down to his secret workshop.

4) He'd show us a Sasquatch robot.

5) We'd maybe have snacks.

6) He'd tell us how he wanted us to help him.

What I Was Not Expecting

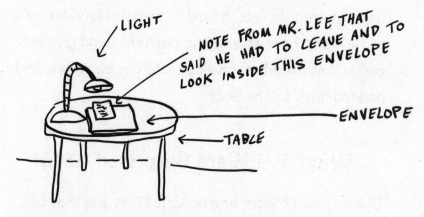

I wasn't the only one surprised. Lewis couldn't believe it either. Where was Mr. Lee?

"Well, that's it," said Lewis. "Forget the crying."

I didn't say anything, but he was right. How could Mr. Lee help us with the Sasquatch if he wasn't even here? I grabbed the envelope, and we walked back outside into the daylight. I don't know why Mr. Lee liked everything so dark and spooky. It was impossible to see in there.

The envelope was bulky and heavier than I

thought it would be. Before I could open it, Lewis tugged on my sleeve and pointed back at the garage.

"Let's go down to the workroom. Maybe Mr. Lee's in there hiding from us."

I nodded. That's exactly the kind of thing Mr. Lee would do—pretend to not be home. He was good at that. In fact, he did it every Halloween, just so he didn't have to see bad costumes and give out candy. I stuffed the envelope into my backpack, and headed back to the door.

What We Were Surprised About

The key didn't work anymore. It fit in the lock, but it wouldn't turn to unlock the door.

DOOR

MAYBE IT'S MAGIC OR SOMETHING.

It was unbelievable. But then, a lot of things about Mr. Lee were that way.

Lewis thumped his head with his fist. "I should have had that idea when we were inside."

Lewis flopped down on the grass. He pulled the plankton paragraph out of his pocket and threw it on the lawn. "Plus, all that work for nothing!"

For a second I thought that maybe we shouldn't be sitting on Mr. Lee's lawn, but looking across the street at my house changed my mind. The curtains were open and I could see Betty dancing around the living room. Only this time it wasn't with a broom—it was with Mom. I sat down next to Lewis. It was safer here. Besides, if we were lucky, maybe Mr. Lee would come out and yell at us.

Lewis was anxious about the envelope, so I let him rip it open. There were three things inside: a note, a phone, and something that looked like a TV remote or a giant game controller. While I was reading the note, Lewis fiddled with the buttons and levers on the controller. Not a good idea, because suddenly a yellow light flashed and the controller started beeping. Lewis dropped it and we both jumped. Was it going to explode?

I studied the note. Maybe there were instructions for the controller. It was hard to concentrate with all the beeping, but neither of us wanted to touch it.

FLASHING LIGHT

The Note

Boys, I had to leave town on an emergency mission. Here is what I need you to do:

1. If anyone in town says they have seen a Sasquatch, please call me immediately at 555-6799. The Sasquatch should stay hidden, but I installed some new software and had to leave before I could test it. Do not worry. The chance of a problem is only .05 percent.

2. If you cannot reach me at 555-6799, do the following: Turn the blue dial on the remote unit to ON. A yellow light will flash and the unit will

beep. Slide the plastic cover to the left, and you will see a map. Follow the map to locate the Sasquatch.

3. Try calling me on the phone provided. The number is 555-6799.

4. Turn the red dial to the OFF position to shut down the Sasquatch.

5. Try calling me on the phone provided. The number is 555-6799.

6. Return home and try calling me on the phone provided until you reach me. The number is 555-6799.

7. If nothing unusual happens, do not call me. I will be returning on Sunday night.

THE NUMBER WE'D NEVER FORGET

555-6799

When I got to the end of the note, Lewis picked up the remote and slid the plastic cover to the left. The beeping stopped. He walked over, grabbed his plankton paragraph, and shoved it back into his pocket. It seemed like we were leaving, but instead of turning toward home, Lewis tapped the remote and said, "Let's go find it."

I should have argued with him, but I didn't. Controlling a Sasquatch robot is a once-in-a-lifetime thing, and even if we were going to get in trouble, it was probably going to be worth it.

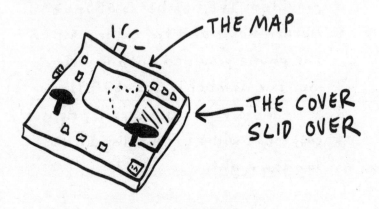

THE MAP

THE COVER
SLID OVER

Sasquatch Hunt

I stuck the note and the phone in my backpack, and then Lewis and I studied the map. It wasn't hard to follow, and in a few minutes we were on the same trail where we'd first seen the alien.

I looked over Lewis's shoulder. "Twenty minutes to go."

Lewis stopped walking. "How do you know?"

I pointed to a small square at the bottom of the remote. Every second the numbers changed, like a countdown on a video game.

EDGE OF CONTROLLER

NUMBER COUNTDOWN

"Oh," said Lewis, and he started walking again. I could tell he was disappointed and kind of wishing he'd noticed it. He held the controller out for me. "Here, do you want to hold it?"

I shook my head. "It's OK. You use it, but when we get to the Sasquatch, I want a turn."

Lewis nodded and stepped off the trail. This was not going to be easy. Now we had to make our own path through bushes that had thousands of prickles. I held my backpack in front of me like a shield. It helped. After a couple of minutes, Lewis

gave me the controller and we traded places. I had
protection. It was easier if I went first.

Making a trail through prickles is not easy. We'd
been walking for about five minutes when we
came across the STAY ON INN sign lying in the bushes.
It was the sign from Lewis's family's motel.
Someone had pulled it off its post and dropped it
here, in the middle of nowhere. When we'd first
found it, we'd tried to move it, but that was
impossible. It weighed a ton. Even Lewis's parents

couldn't figure how to get it out. The trail was too small for a truck, and the sign was too heavy to carry. Lewis kicked it as we walked by, and then he turned around and gave it an extra kick. I knew why—it was because of Officer Gary.

WHAT OFFICER GARY TOLD LEWIS'S PARENTS WHEN THEY ASKED FOR HELP WITH THEIR SIGN

I CAN'T HELP YOU WITH THE SIGN.

IT SAYS RIGHT HERE IN THE MANUAL THAT A CRIME HAS TO BE REPORTED WITHIN 24 HOURS.

THAT SIGN HAS BEEN IN THE WOODS FOR MONTHS.

The timer said we still had eighteen minutes and twenty-three seconds to go. I made an acrostic to kill time. It was better than thinking about how long this was taking.

STRANGE CREATURE

A FAKE OR REAL?

SUPER MYSTERIOUS

QUICKLY HIDES

UNIQUE

ALWAYS FURRY

TO CATCH ONE IS IMPOSSIBLE

CAN RUN FAST

HAS ARMS LIKE AN APE

Sasquatch Dreams

We were getting close.

I turned and looked at Lewis. "Only seven minutes and forty-nine seconds to go."

Lewis nodded. "Do you think the Sasquatch could carry me?"

My brain made a picture. I laughed.

Lewis poked me. "What's so funny about riding on a Sasquatch?"

"Like a baby," I said, and then I laughed again. Of course he had no idea what I was talking about.

He poked me again. "What baby? I could hold the controller while riding on its shoulders."

Now I had a new picture in my brain. I nodded. That sounded like fun. If Lewis was going to ride the Sasquatch, I was too.

The Surprise About the Sasquatch

We smelled it before we saw it. At first we weren't sure if it really was the Sasquatch that was smelly, but once we got closer, we could tell—it had to be. And Sasquatch stink was the worst smell I had ever smelled in my whole life.

"AAAWWWWWW!" I held my nose.

Lewis covered his face with his hands and made a gagging noise. "EEEEWWWWW! Now I know why Mr. Lee doesn't keep it in his studio."

It was disgusting! Even with my nose plugged I could still smell it, and now I could practically taste

70

it too. I almost threw up. I turned and stumbled back the way we'd come. Lewis followed close behind. Finally, when we could breathe again, I stopped. The air was still smelly, but at least we weren't choking.

"Where is it?" asked Lewis.

I pointed to a small furry blob in the distance. All we could see was its shoulders and head.

"But we can hardly see it," complained Lewis.

I shook my head. I wasn't going any closer.

Robot Sasquatch

I studied the controller. Now was the time to make the Sasquatch move.

ONE LEVER PROBABLY CONTROLS THE ARMS AND THE OTHER ONE CONTROLS THE LEGS.

Lewis waved his hand in front of his face. "Why does it stink so much?"

I shrugged. "Maybe it's to keep people away, like a skunk's smell."

Lewis plugged his nose. "Well, it works."

I pointed to the left lever. Should I push it? Lewis nodded. I counted down in my head—five, four, three, two, one—and then I slowly moved it back and forth. Suddenly the Sasquatch was waving.

"IT WORKS! IT WORKS!" shouted Lewis. He jumped up and down.

I moved the lever again, this time faster, and the Sasquatch waved again—faster too.

Lewis yanked my arm. "MY TURN!"

When something is fun, it's not easy to give it up. But I made myself let Lewis have a turn. It was only fair.

What Was Not Good

I don't know what Lewis pushed, but instantly the Sasquatch was gone. We waited for a few seconds to see if it would come back, but it didn't. Had it run off? I looked at the map. The light on the map was flashing right where it'd been before. There was only one explanation: he was on the ground.

I pointed to the lever. "Move it again. Try to make him stand up."

Lewis pushed and pulled, but nothing happened. There was no Sasquatch.

He looked worried. "Did I break it?"

I shook my head. "Maybe we're just pressing things in the wrong order."

Lewis wiggled the levers back and forth. "What do you think he's doing?"

I didn't answer, but my brain made a picture.

SASQUATCH MAKING A "DIRT" ANGEL ON THE GROUND

Lewis wanted to go closer and look at the Sasquatch, but I couldn't do it. I made a choking sound. "I'll die! I won't be able to breathe!"

For a second I thought he might leave and go closer without me, but he changed his mind. "Yeah, you're right. Plus, it's getting dark, and if we're going to ride it, we'll need clothes we can throw away, because being near that thing will smell us up."

Nothing stops Lewis. I couldn't believe he was still thinking about riding the Sasquatch.

"Don't worry," said Lewis. "I have a plan! Tomorrow morning's the ride. You in?"

Riding a giant stink bomb?

I smiled. "You bet."

Before we left, we turned the red button to OFF—just to be safe. That made me think about Mr. Lee. Would he be surprised that we'd tested the robot?

GIVING US THE CONTROLLER WAS LIKE ASKING A DOG NOT TO TOUCH A BONE

Lewis Thinks of Everything

On the way home, Lewis explained his plan for the next day. I couldn't believe he'd just thought of it, because it was perfect and genius. I would have bowed down to him, but there were prickles everywhere, and I didn't want to get poked in the eye.

"Protective clothing! That's key," said Lewis. "Every part of our bodies has to be covered. We don't want that stink on us."

THE CLOTHES THAT WE NEED TO WEAR FOR RIDING THE SASQUATCH

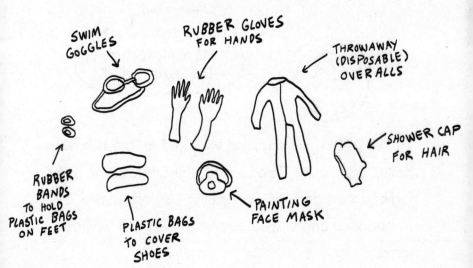

SWIM GOGGLES

RUBBER GLOVES FOR HANDS

THROWAWAY (DISPOSABLE) OVERALLS

SHOWER CAP FOR HAIR

RUBBER BANDS TO HOLD PLASTIC BAGS ON FEET

PLASTIC BAGS TO COVER SHOES

PAINTING FACE MASK

The only thing I had from the list was swim goggles. Lewis said not to worry—he had everything else.

That part wasn't so true because the more we talked about the plan, the less perfect it became. It turned out that he didn't have everything we needed. Lewis is lucky that I'm the kind of person who saves birthday money because we needed to buy disposable overalls. I had forty-six dollars and thirty-nine cents. Hopefully that would be enough. In case it wasn't, Lewis said he was going to look in the cushions of his couch at home. It was hard to believe, but the only money Lewis had was a lucky penny.

He offered it up, but I said, "You should keep it. It's probably worth more for luck."

YAY! I'M WORTH MORE THAN ONE CENT!

"We can buy everything we need at the hardware store," said Lewis. "It opens at eight, but come over earlier so we can get everything else organized."

I nodded and waved, and then we both walked home.

Thinking about riding a Sasquatch is the kind of thing that can keep you up all night. I finally had to do an acrostic to relax and get myself to fall asleep.

FASTER THAN WALKING

UP IN THE AIR

NO ONE HAS DONE THIS BEFORE

RACING THROUGH THE WOODS

IS IT SCARY?

DEFINITELY DANGEROUS

EXCITED TO TRY IT

Saturday

Normally Mom and Dad don't get up early on Saturdays, but when I walked into the kitchen, Dad was already there, eating a muffin. He handed me one. It was blueberry, my favorite. I was going to pack some of those for later.

I took a bite and tried to pretend everything was normal. It was good acting, because my insides were like popcorn.

GOOD THING DAD CAN'T SEE HOW EXCITED I AM.

← ME TRYING TO LOOK NORMAL

It's not easy to eat when you're excited, but I choked down the muffin, then asked Dad for a ride to Lewis's house.

He nodded and pointed out the window. "I need to get that gutter fixed before I go to work. It's going to rain tonight."

I looked to where he was pointing. Part of the gutter was hanging down in front of the window.

Dad shook his head. "Darn squirrels. They've built a nest on the roof again."

I looked at him but didn't say anything. This

was tricky. I had to look interested, but not too interested, or he'd ask me to stay home and help.

While Dad was finishing his breakfast, I packed up the muffins and then followed him out to the car. He was complaining about something not being open, but I didn't pay attention. I had my own things to think about. Dad owns a sporting goods store, and he's always grumbling about work. Mostly I think he just wishes that people around here were more sporty and bought lots of sporting equipment.

THIS TOWN IS FULL OF LAYABOUTS.*

* DAD'S WORD FOR LAZY PEOPLE

On the way to Lewis's house, we drove by the hardware store. It felt weird knowing I'd be sneaking back there in an hour.

As we passed it, Dad said, "Why can't they open a little earlier? What if people have an emergency gutter to fix?"

This time I was listening, and now I knew exactly what he was talking about. Dad was going to go to the hardware store too! What if he saw me there? He'd ask all kinds of questions—things like, Why are you buying disposable overalls? That would be impossible to answer. I had to stop him from going, but how? I tried to think of something good, but all I could come up with were dumb ideas.

DON'T GO TO THE HARDWARE STORE. YOU'LL BE... TRAMPLED BY ELEPHANTS.

MARTIANS ARE GOING TO INVADE.

BEARS WILL BE *THERE*.

Lewis's House

When we pulled up to the motel, Lewis and Red were standing out front waiting for me. Dad stopped the car and I jumped out. Usually Dad asks me about my plans for the day, but today he didn't even wave good-bye.

Lewis took one look at me and asked, "What's wrong?"

My face wasn't hiding the bad news. I told him about Dad and the hardware store.

"That's a problem," said Lewis, and he shook his head.

I started to shake my head too, but then stopped. I had a new idea. "Red can do it. He can pretend your dad sent him. We'll give him a list and my money, and he can buy what we need. We'll go with him, but we'll hide in the bushes or something."

Lewis slapped me on the back. "Excellent! This is going to be the best class project ever. We might even win the best scarecrow prize." Lewis smiled big, like he was trying to tell me something, but he didn't have to work so hard. I knew what he was doing. He was tricking his brother—making up a cover story so we didn't have to tell him the truth. We'd done it before. Poor Red. He didn't have a clue.

"Yay!" screamed Red.

He bounced up and down. He loved helping us. Lewis pointed to the motel. "Let's get the other stuff."

I followed Lewis and Red inside to a room I'd never seen before. It was piled high with boxes and tons of junk.

"We aren't supposed to be in here," whispered Lewis. "So don't knock anything over."

That wasn't going to be easy—there was stuff everywhere. For safety, I waited by the door. Lewis and Red disappeared. When they came back, Lewis had his arms full and Red was holding a paintbrush. Lewis cleared a spot by the door and dumped everything onto the floor.

Red pointed to the face masks. "Can I have one?"

For a second Lewis looked like he might say no, but then he disappeared behind some boxes and came back with another mask.

"Don't let anyone see this," he said.

Red nodded. He was grinning like a crazy person.

The Hardware Store

We found a great hiding spot around the back, behind some bushes.

Lewis went over the things-to-buy list with Red. He was really serious.

"We don't want any mistakes," said Lewis. "So concentrate."

There were only two things on the list—disposable overalls and rubber gloves—but it was a good idea to be careful. We didn't want a mix-up.

Right before Red left, we gave him some last-minute instructions. Just talking about it made me feel nervous.

So far we hadn't seen Dad's car, but the hardware store had just opened, so he could show up any second. When it was time to go, I gave Red my birthday money and the extra fifty-six cents from Lewis's sofa. We watched Red walk to the front of the building. For some reason, he looked even smaller than normal.

Lewis must have been worried, because he said, "If he's not back here in ten minutes, I'm going in."

I was about to say, *Good plan*, but I couldn't

speak. I grabbed Lewis's arm and pointed to the parking lot. There in front of us was Dad getting out of his car.

What a Bad Feeling Would Look Like if You Drew It

What a Really Bad Feeling Would Look Like if You Drew It

I held my stomach. Both those bad feelings were inside me, doing some kind of stupid dance, like Betty's cha-cha. It made me feel sick.

What Took Forever

Ten minutes can seem like a long time if you're waiting and worrying. Lewis was about to sneak around to the front of the store when suddenly we saw Red running toward us. As soon as I stood up, he stopped and looked down at the ground.

Lewis motioned him over. Red had a bag with him, so that was good news, but I had a feeling there was bad news too.

The First Thing Red Said to Me

"Don't get mad."

Usually when someone says that, it's a bad sign.

Red handed me the bag of supplies and the envelope with my money.

"Someone helped me," he said. "But you're not going to like the someone." And then, before I

could even guess who he was talking about, he said,
"It was your dad."

I didn't mean to, but my whisper-shouting made
Red almost cry. While Lewis tried to calm him
down, I made an acrostic to punish myself.

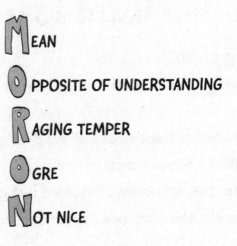

Red and Dad

I was expecting the news to be awful, but it wasn't. Dad had just helped him find the best deals and save the most money—and it was *my* money he was saving. I added the word *total* to my punishment. I deserved it. I was a total moron for getting mad.

TOO MUCH WHISPER-YELLING

OUT OF CONTROL

TREATED RED BADLY

ANGRY FOR NO REASON

LETTING RED FEEL BAD

It's not easy to say you're sorry, but I made myself do it. After that, Red felt better. He took the bag from me to show us what he'd bought.

He held up a package. "It's coveralls because they were cheaper than overalls, and the gloves were on sale for ninety-nine cents. And look! They're even kind of fancy."

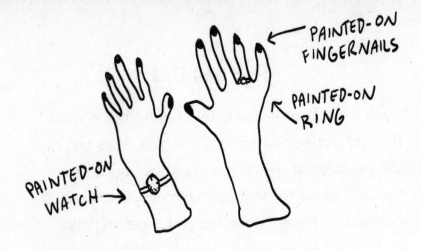

PAINTED-ON FINGERNAILS

PAINTED-ON RING

PAINTED-ON WATCH →

GIRL GLOVES! I didn't want to wear those! I looked at Lewis.

He shrugged. "No one's going to see us."

He was right, and when I counted my leftover money, I felt even better. I still had twenty-five dollars and change. It was way more than I was expecting. Girl gloves were worth it.

Lewis let Red wear a pair of the gloves on the walk back to the motel. He ran ahead of us, jumping and laughing like this was the best day of his life.

Sasquatch Trail

After we dropped off Red, we packed up everything and headed to the woods. Was Lewis as excited as

I was? He was walking extra fast, so I guessed the answer was yes.

In less than twenty minutes, we were back where we'd been the day before. I covered my nose. The Sasquatch was still smelly. Now was the time. Lewis and I put on our special outfits.

Two Reasons to Be Glad

1) We had the outfits.
2) No one could see us in our outfits.

The only bad part was that the face masks made it hard to understand each other. We practiced a bit. Talking slow and loud helped.

SHOWER CAP

SWIM GOGGLES

COVERALLS

FACE MASK

FANCY GLOVES

PLASTIC BAGS OVER SHOES

The Sasquatch

Lewis turned the red button to ON and walked
forward. I followed close behind, and then we
found it, the Sasquatch. It was on the ground,
lying on its side, not as big as I'd imagined.
Lewis pushed the lever on the right side of the
controller, and the Sasquatch moved its legs.
The faster Lewis pushed the lever, the faster
the legs moved, until it almost looked like the
Sasquatch was running. Dirt was flying
everywhere. If he hadn't been so big and moving
so fast, it would have been funny. But being there
and standing so close to the giant stinky beast
was the opposite of funny. It was kind of scary.

← LOOKING DOWN
ON THE SASQUATCH
AS IT RUNS ON ITS
SIDE IN THE DIRT

I pulled my face mask tighter. Sasquatch smell was not something I wanted to experience. And definitely not this close.

"What do you think this does?" asked Lewis. He was pointing to a button on the controller, but before I could answer, he pushed it. Suddenly the Sasquatch was on its feet standing over us.

WE ARE BOTH SCREAMING BUT NO ONE CAN TELL →

SCARED EYES

I screamed and fell back into Lewis, knocking the controller out of his hands and up into the air. Where it landed was not good.

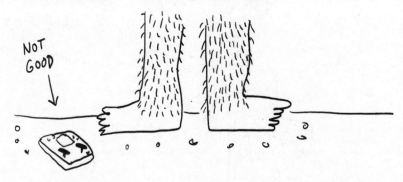

NOT GOOD ↓

What Was Different

The Sasquatch looked a whole lot bigger now that he was standing up.

What We Did for Twenty Minutes

We walked around the Sasquatch and studied him. Lewis even poked him. I wasn't sure that was a good idea, but after he did it and nothing happened, I did it too. For some reason it was a lot less scary than touching Mr. Lee's other robot, the alien. I don't know why, but the Sasquatch seemed less creepy. There was something about the alien that bugged me. It was only a robot, but still, I didn't trust it. Even thinking about it made me shudder.

YOU NEVER KNOW WHAT I MIGHT DO.

How Lewis Surprised Me

He picked up the controller and handed it to me. "You go first," said Lewis.

I couldn't tell if he was being nice or if he thought I'd do a better job, but whatever the reason, I didn't say no. I couldn't wait to get the Sasquatch moving. Before I pushed or moved anything, I studied the controls. There were a lot of buttons, and to do things right, we needed to test out each one of them. If Mom had been here, I knew exactly what I would have said.

Some Things That Are Fun to Make a Sasquatch Do

SASQUATCH JACKS
(LIKE JUMPING JACKS)

SASQUATCH SQUATS

SASQUATCH STAND
(LIKE A HEADSTAND)

Lewis and I took turns, and after a while we were both pretty good at making the Sasquatch do whatever we could think of. The only thing we didn't try was riding it. There are just three words to describe riding a Sasquatch: SUPER CRAZY DANGEROUS!

Five Ways to Die by Sasquatch Riding

1) If you fell off, it could step on you.
2) You could get your head knocked off by a branch while it was walking or running.
3) You could drop the controller, lose control of it, and then smash into a tree.

4) If the Sasquatch tripped and fell, you'd be squashed under its body.
5) If your face mask fell off, you'd die from Sasquatch-stink inhalation.

Thinking of them made me feel a lot better about staying on the ground.

Sasquatch Skill

There was one thing about the Sasquatch that I hadn't expected: it was super strong. Lewis had the idea to see if it could hold things. The first thing we tried to lift was a giant log. We couldn't budge it, but the Sasquatch picked it up without any problem. It could pick up anything. Its hands worked like giant clamps—opening and then snapping shut to hold things. We picked up a bunch of stuff—giant rocks, super big logs, bears...Well, we didn't actually test bears, but if there'd been one, I'm sure the Sasquatch could have done it.

What Makes Time Go By Fast

Controlling a robot. When Lewis and I finally stopped for a break, it was already two o'clock. We were starving. It's not easy to forget about lunch. You have to be doing something really fun for that to happen. The only bad part about eating was that we had to take our masks off. There was no way we could do that next to the Sasquatch, so we walked back to where we'd been the day before. I sat down and pulled off my mask. One breath later, I was gagging and frantically trying to get it back on.

"Ahhhh!"

"IT'S YOU!" shouted Lewis. His face mask was off too. He turned away from me, threw up, and then somehow got his mask back on.

Me? Why was it me? And then I knew. It wasn't me—it was both of us. We smelled like Sasquatch stink. Even with my mask on, I could smell it. I tightened the strap, but it still felt loose. I fiddled with it but couldn't get it any tighter.

I sat with Lewis while we waited for him to feel better. My stomach was rumbling, but I tried to ignore it. How could my body want to eat when everything smelled so bad? It was a stinky mystery.

I made up an acrostic to kill time.

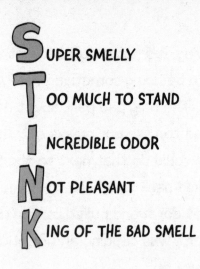

SUPER SMELLY

TOO MUCH TO STAND

INCREDIBLE ODOR

NOT PLEASANT

KING OF THE BAD SMELL

Once Lewis felt better, we decided to forget about lunch. Instead, we walked back to the Sasquatch. We had something important to do.

New Rule

Lewis and I had a new rule: if you see something unusual, take a picture of it. When you learn a rule by experience, you never forget it. If we'd had a photo of our alien sighting, things would have turned out different, because people believe pictures more than they believe words. We weren't going to make that mistake with the Sasquatch. This time I had my camera, and we were going to take pictures—lots of them.

CAMERA TALKING

I CAN CHANGE PEOPLE'S MINDS. I HAVE THAT KIND OF POWER.

I let Lewis go first since he'd actually thrown up. That kind of suffering deserves a reward.

Lewis likes to make things complicated, so of course the photo he wanted was dangerous. I was nervous about it, but I didn't try to stop him. I had one goal—take it fast so he could get down.

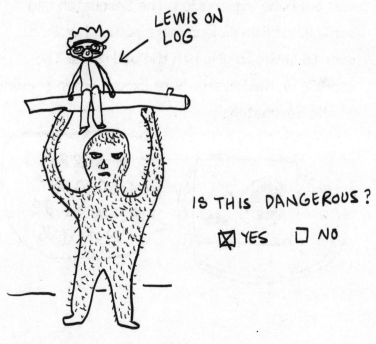

LEWIS ON LOG

IS THIS DANGEROUS?
☒ YES ☐ NO

When Lewis was ready, I pointed the camera at him and pushed the button to take the photo, but nothing happened. I looked the camera over. It seemed fine. Then by accident, I pushed the button while it was pointed at my foot—*click!* It took a picture. I waved at Lewis for him to get ready, but when I pointed the camera and pushed the button, the same thing happened again.

I shook it. "Stupid camera!"

Of course, that didn't help. I pointed it at my foot—*click.* At my face—*click.* At the ground—*click.* At Lewis and the Sasquatch—nothing. There was only one explanation. The Sasquatch had some kind of invisible camera power. I walked over to Lewis to give him the bad news. The camera worked everywhere except when pointing at the Sasquatch.

I'M SORRY, I JUST DON'T SEEM TO BE WORKING.

Lewis wasn't mad like I thought he'd be. Instead, he shook his head and said, "Mr. Lee thinks of everything."

I didn't say anything back, because mostly I was just glad that he let me lower the log down so he could get off.

What Would Have Been Fun

To march around town with the Sasquatch. But of course we couldn't. Still, it was fun to imagine.

My stomach was grumbling again. It was four o'clock. I showed Lewis the time.

"Should we go?"

The Sasquatch was fun, but I'd had enough for one day. Lewis and I walked back to the safe spot and took off our outfits. We kept the masks on and walked even farther away before we took those off too. We hid the masks by the STAY ON INN sign. We were leaving lucky. Nothing bad had happened and no one had seen us. And if we didn't tell Mr. Lee, maybe he'd never know. A second later, I shook my head. No, that was wrong. Mr. Lee would know—he probably had some kind of sensor on the robot.

I tapped Lewis on the arm. "Should we tell Mr. Lee about the Sasquatch?"

Lewis smiled. It was his sneaky smile—the one that meant he was thinking about something that had nothing to do with my question.

Lewis's Old Plan, Plus a New Plan

WE NEED TO LET MARCUS SEE THE SASQUATCH.

OLD PLAN

I BET THE SASQUATCH CAN CARRY THE STAY ON INN MOTEL SIGN BACK TO OUR MOTEL.

NEW PLAN

This was not good news, Now there were two things to worry about. "We need Marcus Wolver," said Lewis, "and the motel needs the sign."

How were we going to get that huge sign to the motel without anyone seeing us? And what about Marcus Wolver? It wasn't like we could say, *Hey, Marcus, stand here and watch the woods for fifteen minutes.* How were Marcus and the Sasquatch going to be in the same place at the same time?

Lewis had answers for everything.

"We'll put the sign up at night. Marcus has a violin lesson on Sunday afternoons. He told me he always takes a shortcut near the woods. We'll just wait for him, have the Sasquatch jump up, and then we're done."

I nodded, but I wasn't done. "How do we get the Sasquatch to the right place without anyone seeing it?"

Lewis thought for a moment. "We hide him there the night before."

Finally, after a bunch more questions, I had to say yes. The plan wasn't perfect, but it was better than doing nothing. Doing nothing meant Lewis would move away and that couldn't happen. We had to try.

I didn't think it was possible, but needing Marcus Wolver made me not like him even more.

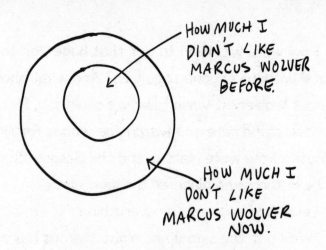

HOW MUCH I DIDN'T LIKE MARCUS WOLVER BEFORE.

HOW MUCH I DON'T LIKE MARCUS WOLVER NOW.

Sneaking Out at Night

Getting out of Lewis's house in the middle of the night was different from getting out of my house in the middle of the night. My house was trickier. I had to get past Betty.

THREE THINGS I HAVE TO DO

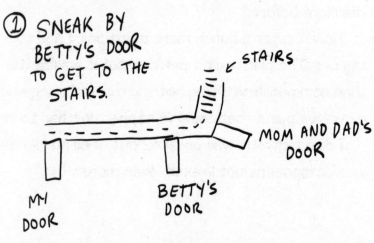

① SNEAK BY BETTY'S DOOR TO GET TO THE STAIRS.

STAIRS

MOM AND DAD'S DOOR

MY DOOR

BETTY'S DOOR

② SNEAK PAST THE KITCHEN— SOMEONE COULD BE SNACKING.

③ SNEAK OUT THE BROKEN WINDOW IN THE BASEMENT.

The Midnight Plan

"We'll leave at midnight with flashlights," said Lewis.

It took a while to decide where to meet. Lewis wanted to meet in the woods at the start of the trail, but I wasn't brave enough for that.

Even walking in the woods would be scary. "What about bears?" I asked.

"We'll put on our Sasquatch outfits," said Lewis. He held his nose. "No bear will come near us."

I hadn't thought of that. It was true. Bears probably didn't like Sasquatch stink either.

Finally we agreed on a meeting place. Lewis was grumpy because it was out of his way, but it was good for me.

"Okay," I said. "I'll see you at midnight, in the bushes, beside my broken basement window."

Everything was set. And finding our outfits at night would be easy—all we needed was our noses.

THOSE CLOTHES SMELL DISGUSTING!

Before we left, I asked Lewis one more thing.

"Bring Red's face mask. Mine is loose, and it feels like it might fall off."

Then Lewis high-fived me.

"For what we've done and what we're going to do," said Lewis.

I slapped his hand, but I wasn't as excited as he was. Sneaking out at night? Walking in the woods after midnight? It was more scary than exciting. On the walk home, I made an acrostic.

BEARS SCARE ME

I CAN'T WALK ALONE

GIANT SHADOWS

BIG NOISES IN THE DARK

ANYTHING COULD BE OUT THERE

BETTER TO STAY HOME

YOU CAN GO WITHOUT ME

Why I Was Lucky

When I got home, Mom and Betty were out shopping for dance shoes, Dad was eating his dinner in front of the TV, and mine was on the stove. Dinner was turkey chili—not my favorite, but there was cornbread, and that made up for it.

"Help yourself," Dad said. I grabbed a plate full of cornbread and was about to head upstairs. Normally I'm not allowed to eat in my room, but tonight no one was around to stop me.

"What the heck have you been doing?"

I froze. It was Dad, but he sounded funny. I turned around. He was holding his nose. He took a few steps back and waved his hand in front of his face.

"What a stink! You'd better shower, and throw those clothes in the laundry basket in the basement before your mother gets home."

I nodded.

Dad mumbled and complained all the way back to the living room. As soon as he was gone, I ran upstairs. How come I couldn't smell the stink? Was I used to it?

After eating, I took a shower with extra soap and threw my clothes in the basement. Hopefully Mom wouldn't notice anything.

Betty

It wasn't hard to stay up until midnight, mostly because after Mom and Betty got home, there was lots of clomping and stomping going on in Betty's room. Peeking in to see what she was doing was a big mistake. She made me sit on her bed for twenty minutes and be her audience.

Every part of it was torture. The listening...

...and the watching.

But I lied and said she was good, because Betty has other moves that she really is good at (though they have nothing to do with dancing).

The only lucky part was that she didn't make me dance with her. It wasn't a compliment, but she said, "You're too shrimpy."

Why Water Was My Friend

Dancing = thirsty

and

Drinking water = having to go to the bathroom

Betty stopped dancing and pointed at me. "Stay here. I'll be back in a minute."

I made myself nod, but the second she was in the bathroom I was gone.

I wasn't so sure about the power of my door sign, but it worked. Betty didn't come in, and a few minutes later I heard her dancing again. Mom finally made her stop around ten thirty.

MY EARS SAYING THANK YOU

Midnight Escape

I was dressed and ready to go by eleven o'clock. I spent the last hour pacing back and forth and looking out the window to see if I could spot Lewis. What if something bad happened? What if he wouldn't come? Then what? After about ten minutes, I realized I was worrying about the wrong thing. What I really should have been worrying about was Lewis actually showing up.

At eleven fifty-five, I took one last look out the window and then slowly opened my door. I listened. All was quiet. Everyone was sleeping. My biggest worry was Betty. Could I get by her room without her hearing me? She has a lot of super skills, and hearing is one of them.

Dad says she has ears like a bat. Not a great compliment, but Betty doesn't care. She turns everything into a compliment.

I was carrying my shoes—socks are quieter—and my backpack. To be extra safe, I held my breath as I passed her room. It was a half relief to get to the top of the stairs, and then a full relief when I made it to the bottom. Home free! And then I turned the corner...and walked right into Betty.

She glared at me.

"Well, if you're looking for the cornbread, you're out of luck." She popped something into her mouth. "This is the last piece."

Suddenly, her eyes widened.

"Hey, you're not wearing pajamas. What are you doing? Are you sneaking out?"

Before I could say anything, she yanked me into the kitchen and backed me up against the counter. Her finger poked at my chest—hard.

"You better tell me what's going on! And now! START TALKING!"

There wasn't time to tell her the whole story, but I got the important stuff out—Mr. Lee, Sasquatch robot, helping Lewis with his motel. And then I begged.

Betty Eyes

Betty has two kinds of eyes—normal eyes and snake eyes. Snake eyes always mean trouble, and right now she had snake eyes.

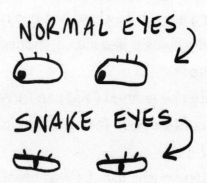

Was she going to wake up Mom and Dad? I slumped against the counter.

The Surprise

Betty grabbed my arm and pulled me toward the basement door. Was she going to throw me down the stairs? Kill me? I tried to get away, but that only made her hold on tighter.

"Stop squirming!" she snapped. "Lewis is waiting and we'll be late."

I couldn't believe it. "You're coming?"

She whacked me on the back. "Now MOVE! Of course I'm coming. I wouldn't let you two runts go into the woods alone. Plus, I like Lewis. And the whole robot thing is...interesting. How big is it?"

I lifted my arm up to show her, but not holding onto the railing was a bad idea. I tripped and missed a step.

"Watch it!" she snarled. "You can't even get down the stairs without falling. It's a good thing I'm coming."

I didn't say anything, but I was pretty sure she was wrong.

Supplies

While we were in the basement, I grabbed some things Betty would need and shoved them into my backpack. There wasn't much choice, but some protection was better than nothing. She'd thank me later—or not.

CHEF'S HAT

SKI GLOVES

SAFETY GOGGLES →

← WIZARD ROBE FROM HALLOWEEN

Betty was standing on a chair under the broken window, waving at me. She was probably scowling too, but it was too dark to tell.

"Stop messing around! Let's go."

I thought about throwing her stuff out of my backpack. But I didn't. Why? Because I'm nicer than she is. A second later she was gone, and the window banged against the wall. I scrambled after her. I had to catch up. Betty does not wait.

Lewis's Surprise

When I got outside, Lewis and Betty were standing by the bushes.

"I was hoping you'd come," whispered Lewis.

Betty smiled and said something I couldn't hear. Gross! Was he flirting with her?

Lewis saw me walking toward him. He held up the extra face mask. "See, I remembered. Good thing I brought another one." He handed it to Betty.

She made a face. "What's this for?"

"It's a surprise," said Lewis, and he smiled at me.

SO HOW BIG IS THIS ROBOT?

DOES IT HAVE FLASHING LIGHTS ON IT?

CAN YOU MAKE IT DO ANYTHING COOL?

← FACE MASK

Betty had a lot of questions, but Lewis and I pretty much ignored them. She'd find out soon enough.

Getting Ready

We got to the STAY ON INN sign without any trouble and picked up our face masks. I'd been right about finding our special outfits—we smelled them before we saw them. Betty held her nose and complained about a skunk.

"It's not a skunk, it's a Sasquatch," said Lewis, and he pointed to her face mask. "You should probably put that on." I was mad about Betty getting the good face mask, but once we were all dressed, I felt better. She looked ridiculous.

Lewis leaned over and whispered, "What's she supposed to be? Some kind of wizard chef?"

It was hard not to burst out laughing.

Traveling the rest of the way wasn't hard for us, but Betty was having trouble. Her wizard robe was like a prickles magnet.

Ta-Da—Sasquatch!

When we got close to the Sasquatch, Lewis handed me the remote. We hadn't talked about who would work the Sasquatch, but we both knew who was better at it—me. I pushed some buttons and levers, and then suddenly there he was. I heard a scream and a gasp from behind me. It was Betty. I imagined what she was thinking.

When I turned to look at her, she had only three things to say: "It's too big," "It's dirty," and "Let's get this over with."

"Right down to business. I like that," said Lewis. "Let's go."

He didn't seem to get Betty at all. Was he faking it, or did he not see her evil side? I marched the Sasquatch ahead and we followed behind. I should have been enjoying this part, but all I could think was, *Too big? What did she mean by that?*

It was harder to find the STAY ON INN sign on the way back, probably because the Sasquatch was walking in front of us. We should have marked the spot. I parked the Sasquatch, and Lewis and I looked for the sign. Betty wasn't any help. She just sat on a log and said her outfit wasn't suitable for off-path wandering. To stop her from complaining, I let her play with the remote.

FINE!
I PROMISE
I'LL ONLY
MOVE THE
ARMS.

I wasn't sure if I could trust her, but she surprised me and kept her promise. After about ten minutes, Lewis finally found the sign.

Getting the Sasquatch to pick it up was not as easy as I thought it would be. I had to find a good place for it to clamp onto the sign without crushing it. It seemed like forever, but I got it to work.

The Sasquatch lifted the sign into the air. "AWESOME!" Lewis jumped up and pumped his fist.

Betty didn't say anything. I don't think she cared one way or the other.

The walk to the motel was almost boring—just us following the Sasquatch. Twenty minutes later, we were there.

"So, Lewis, how about a tour?" asked Betty.

I made a gagging sound, but I was lucky that she ignored me. She probably just thought I was choking in my mask.

While Lewis showed Betty around, I maneuvered the Sasquatch over to the two posts in the ground that would hold the sign. It took five tries to get the two holes in the sign positioned over the two posts. It would have been easier if Lewis had been holding a flashlight to help me see, but he was off entertaining Betty. Still, I was glad she wasn't there. The sign made a horrible screeching noise as it slipped into place. I was sure everyone would hear it, but the motel stayed dark.

I parked the Sasquatch behind a tree and sat down to rest. This was definitely not like playing a video game. Video games never made me tired. A few minutes later, Lewis and Betty were back.

"WHOA!" said Lewis. "That is beautiful!"

Even Betty seemed impressed.

BOTTOM ALL RIPPED AND TORN FROM THE PRICKLES

YOU'RE REALLY GOOD WITH THAT THING.

It was probably the nicest compliment she'd ever given me. I was glad it was dark out and I was wearing the mask because, even though I didn't want to, I think I was kind of blushing.

Sasquatch Baby

I was glad the hard part was over. Now all we had to do was drop off the Sasquatch at the meeting point with Marcus. Halfway there, Lewis stopped me.

"I want to ride it," he said.

I couldn't believe it. "On its shoulders?"

"No, like a baby," said Lewis.

I thought he was joking, but he looked serious.

"It's the only safe way."

Lewis loved it, and after his turn Betty wanted a ride too. Mostly I think she was just tired of walking in her wizard outfit. No one offered me a turn, but I didn't complain. I was happy with my two feet on the ground. Lewis wasn't as good as I was with the

controller, and I didn't trust Betty. She was the
kind of person who'd have an accident on purpose.

It was almost three in the morning when we
finally got to the Sasquatch drop-off spot. I was
exhausted, and we still had to walk home. Nobody
said a word until Betty and I turned to leave.

"Tomorrow, two o'clock for Marcus," said Lewis,
and then he was gone.

I was glad I didn't have to walk home alone, but
I didn't tell Betty that. You can't trust her with
real feelings. I thought we'd walk quietly like
before, but the second Lewis was out of sight, she
started asking questions.

I answered most of them, but now I was worried. What was she after?

I stopped in the middle of the road. "You're not going to tell anyone, are you? If you do, we'll get in trouble. Even you!"

Betty shook her head. "Don't worry, I can keep a secret." Suddenly she pulled me close and hugged me. At first I thought it was friendly, but it wasn't. Friendly sisters don't say, "Just remember, little brother, you owe me big!"

It wasn't a good way to end a night. Plus, it was starting to rain.

Back Home

Sneaking into the house was easy. Betty took off her Sasquatch outfit and left it on the basement floor, but suddenly she realized something: she was still stinky.

She punched me in the arm. "I'll probably have to throw these sweatpants away, and they're my favorite." She sniffed her arm and made a face. "I call first shower." Two seconds later, she was gone.

Great! Betty's showers were legendary—she'd be in there for decades. I stumbled up to my room and flopped onto my beanbag to wait, but that turned out to be a very bad thing.

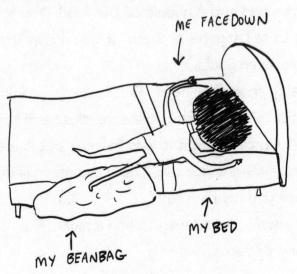

ME FACEDOWN

MY BED

MY BEANBAG

What Is Not a Good Thing to Wake Up To

Yelling!

It took me a few minutes to figure out who was yelling, and then when I did, I got really nervous. It was Mom.

"It's a skunk! Is it still here? MORGAN, GET UP! There's a skunk in your room! Someone get a broom!"

And then Dad was yelling. "I'm coming! I'm sure the screaming scared it away!"

I was up now and standing by my bed. Mom was at the door holding her nose, and I could hear Dad stomping up the stairs. Then Dad was at the door too.

"SWEET HEAVENS! WHAT A STINK! Morgan, get over here!"

I walked toward them, but as soon as I got close they backed away.

"UGH!" Dad waved his hand in front of his face. "IT'S YOU!"

For a second nobody said anything, and then it was all orders and action.

What Happened Next

Mom shouted out a list of what to do and how to do it.

1) Jump in the shower with a garbage bag. Do not turn on the water.
2) Get undressed.
3) Throw your clothes into the garbage bag.
4) Close the garbage bag.

5) Toss the garbage bag onto the floor.

6) Wash your body and hair with lots of soap.

"And look for bite marks," added Mom. "The skunk could have rabies."

While I was in the shower, Mom made Dad check to make sure the skunk was gone and not lying dead in my bed or something.

Of course there wasn't a skunk, but that didn't make it any less terrifying. What was Betty doing? Would she tell them the truth? Would I be in the biggest trouble of my entire life? There was no way to know. The only safe place was the shower. I decided to stay there for as long as I could.

After about thirty minutes, I was wrinkled like an old person and the water was cold. I had to get out. Before I opened the door, I checked for shouting or yelling. There was nothing. I thought I was safe, but that was wrong because the second I stepped out, Betty grabbed me and dragged me into her room.

She'd moved things around. Her chair and lamp were in the middle of the room. She shoved me into the chair. It was just like on TV, when the bad guys make the good guy talk—only her version was more girly looking. But it was still scary, because Betty doing anything was scary.

Betty was mad—wild animal mad. Maybe *she* had rabies! I pushed myself back against the chair, but there was no escape.

GRRRRR!!!

"I don't know how you did it, but because of that stupid Sasquatch, you're getting a whole bedroom makeover! New paint, new carpet, and even a new bed!"

"I am?" That was obviously the wrong thing to say. She picked up her new dance shoe and threw it at my head. I dodged and it grazed my shoulder. That made her madder. I'd never seen her like this. It was frightening, but sort of fascinating too. It made me wonder if people could get mad enough to spontaneously combust.

BETTY DISINTEGRATED—
POOF!
ALL THAT IS LEFT ARE HER SMOLDERING FOOTPRINTS.

"Don't play dumb with me," Betty snarled. "Like you don't know!"

I wanted to shake my head, because I really

didn't know, but I didn't dare move. Suddenly Betty took a step back and turned her head sideways.

"Wait a second. You were in the shower the whole time, so you really don't know."

I thought this might be a good time to talk, but Betty told me to shut up. She's not supposed to use that kind of language, but I let it go.

TWO-PART DEAL!

PART ONE OF THE DEAL. IF YOU CHANGE ROOMS WITH ME, SO I GET THE NEW ROOM, I WON'T SAY ANYTHING ABOUT YOUR SMELLY SASQUATCH!

It was an easy decision, but I didn't answer right away. I pointed to the wall. It was pink and purple. I shook my head. I wasn't living with that.

Betty sighed. "Fine, I'll get Mom and Dad to buy you a can of paint, but that's it. The rest of the money is for me only—and my new room."

I looked around. Everything else was livable. I'd throw out her girly rug, get rid of the princess parts of the bed, and, with my old dresser and desk, it would actually be OK. Plus, her room was bigger.

"OK," I said. "Deal. Now, what's part two?"

PART TWO IS YOU HAVE TO USE ONE OF MR. LEE'S NON-STINKY ROBOTS AND MAKE IT DANCE.

IT'LL BE PERFECT TO HELP ME PRACTICE FOR DYLAN.

What People Only Do in Movies, But What I Did for Real

I fell out of my chair.

What she was asking for was impossible. IMPOSSIBLE! I had to change her mind.

"It's an alien robot. He's ugly and creepy and slimy. You wouldn't want to touch him."

Betty shook her head. "That's not what you said before. If he's slimy, you can dress him up. I don't care about looks. I just need a tall partner to practice with."

She walked over to her desk, grabbed a book, and threw it at me.

"AND YOU'D BETTER PRACTICE! The cha-cha is on page twelve. That robot better have his dance moves down, because if he doesn't..." Betty moved in. Her nose was almost touching mine. "...YOU'LL PAY!"

I could smell her breath. She'd been eating cinnamon bread. I hate cinnamon. I tried to twist my head away, but that only made her poke me.

She had this whole thing planned out. Or did she? Where were we going to practice? Dancing with a big robot was going to take up space. We couldn't do it in the house. Plus, the robot was a secret—no one could see it. Not even Mom or Dad. She probably hadn't thought about that.

I looked up at her. "Where can we practice?" I hoped it was a question that would make her entire plan fall apart.

But I was wrong, because Betty suddenly looked happy.

Betty gave me the snake eyes and marched out of the room. I waited for a few seconds to make sure she wasn't coming back, and then I ran.

Skunk

Mom was at the bottom of the stairway— smiling. Was she happy to see me alive? Rabies-free?

She grabbed me and hugged me. "I'm so glad you and Betty are getting along. That was very generous of you to trade rooms with her. And don't worry about the paint. We'll buy whatever you need. Your friend Lewis can help you paint. It'll be fun."

I nodded and pulled away, but suddenly Dad was there holding my shoulder. "Come in here," he said. "I want to show you something."

I followed him into the kitchen and he pointed to a paper on the counter. He'd drawn a map with little red dots showing the path the skunk had taken. The path looked familiar.

DAD'S MAP OF WHERE THE SKUNK WENT

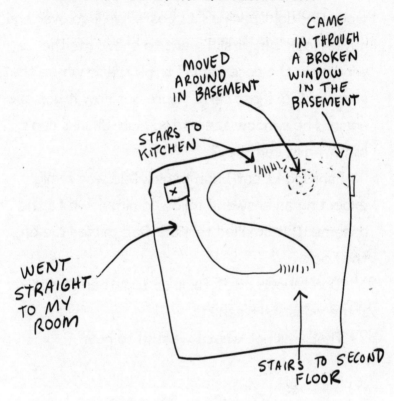

"I called the police to ask about catching it, but they're all busy over at the motel this morning— some kind of hullabaloo with a sign."

I sat down. My legs were shaking.

"Listen to this. In the middle of the night, without anyone seeing anything, someone put that big motel sign—you know, the one in the woods?—right back on its posts. We'll go over and have a look, but first I want to show you the window in the basement. I think that's where the skunk got in. I just can't figure out how it got out again. The window seems too high. Skunks can't climb walls, can they?"

I shrugged, but I don't think Dad was really expecting an answer. I followed him down to the basement. It smelled terrible. Dad patted me on the back.

"Don't worry, we'll fix it up together. I'll get some industrial cleaner."

That was not what I wanted to hear.

The Sign Mystery

I wanted to go straight to Lewis's, but Dad made us stop at the hardware store first to get cleaning supplies and a new window.

The guy behind the counter recognized Dad and said, "Back again?"

That made me glad about yesterday's plan. He couldn't say that to me.

When we got to Lewis's house, there were two police cars out front and a bunch of people standing around the sign.

Dad pointed to it. "Look! There it is."

I should have been proud, but I wasn't. I didn't know this before, but if nervous and proud are in the same body, nervous wins.

Suddenly Lewis was at my car door. He practically pulled me out of the car. Dad and I followed him to a small square of ground blocked off by police tape. Standing inside the square were Officer Gary and a lady in a white coat. She was mixing up some white stuff in a bucket. It looked like oatmeal.

Lewis pointed to a shape on the ground. "That's the only footprint they found. They're going to make a cast of it."

Officer Gary whispered something to the lady, then came over to talk to Dad.

"I don't believe in these things, but there it is." He pointed to the footprint. The lady poured the white stuff on top of it.

Officer Gary put his hands on his hips. His right hand was really close to his gun. I made myself look away. I didn't want him to catch me staring.

He was only talking to Dad, but everyone was listening. "Looks like a right foot. We'd have more prints, but it rained early this morning and washed everything away. This one near the tree was protected. Of course, we'll have to send it off for analysis."

We all looked up at the tree. What if I hadn't parked the Sasquatch under it? I tried not to think about it. It would have changed everything, and not in a good way. I made up a fast acrostic. I had to. The tree had saved us.

THANK YOU FOR BEING HERE

REALLY NEEDED YOU

EVERYONE WILL NOW BELIEVE

EVERYTHING WILL BE OK

Officer Gary pointed to the sign. "And then there's that! I suspect it's those high school kids again. At least this time it's not destruction of property. Did you hear about last month? They put a motorcycle on top of the town fountain." Officer Gary shook his head. "We need more surveillance cameras."

Happy to Unhappy

When no one was looking, Lewis high-fived me. "This will keep our motel busy forever! And Sage and Dave are super excited about the sign."

I tried to fake a smile, but I wasn't very good at it.

Lewis made a guess about why. "Forget Marcus—we don't need him. We're done. And everything worked out even better than we planned, right?"

I shook my head, and then we walked around back. It was time to tell him about Betty.

WOW, SHE'S ALMOST LIKE AN EVIL VILLAIN.

There was only one thing we could do. We had to tell Mr. Lee everything. And then we had to beg him to let us make his alien robot dance with Betty. It seemed impossible.

Broken Window

Even though there was lots of excitement at the motel, Lewis came home with me. I told Dad he wanted to help with the window, but really we wanted to spy on Mr. Lee's house. We needed to talk to him as soon as he got home.

Dad likes showing off his home repair skills, so he was glad to have Lewis along. He even stopped at the deli and bought us a giant sandwich for lunch. Lewis was pretty excited about the sandwich. Mom usually complains about them. She says they smell up the house. But what was worse, sandwich smell or Sasquatch smell?

FILLED WITH MEAT AND CHEESE

It took most of the afternoon to do the fixing and cleaning chores. When we were finished, my room was empty, the window was repaired, and the whole house smelled like fake-lemon cleaner.

Betty had her door closed, but we could hear her practicing. She didn't stop stomping, not even for lunch. Mom said she was determined and that we should be proud of her, but it's impossible to be proud of someone who's about to ruin your life.

Do You Believe?

While we were waiting for Mr. Lee to get home, Lewis and I talked about the Sasquatch. Should I feel guilty about it? Making people believe in something that wasn't real?

When I asked Lewis, he looked surprised, like he hadn't thought of that before. But then he said, "OK, answer this: do you believe in aliens?"

I nodded.

"Even after seeing an alien robot?"

"Yes, because that alien robot has nothing to do with real aliens."

"Exactly," said Lewis. "There are probably real Sasquatches all around here. If you believe, you believe. If you don't, you don't."

I wasn't sure I totally understood what he was saying, but it made me feel better. After all, it was only one footprint. How much could that change?

Perfect Timing?

Lewis and I decided to wait for Mr. Lee at his house. That way we wouldn't miss him. I opened our front door to head out, and—surprise!— Mr. Lee was standing right in front of me.

"Come!" said Mr. Lee, and he turned and walked back to his house.

Lewis and I followed him across the street. Was he mad? Did he know? Were we in big trouble? I had a feeling the answer to all those questions was going to be yes.

TOO LATE TO CHANGE ANYTHING

REALLY SCARED

OUR LIVES COULD BE OVER

UNCOMFORTABLE

BE BRAVE

LIE OR TELL THE TRUTH?

EVERYTHING WILL NOT BE OK

Mr. Lee opened his garage door and walked to the back. Lewis and I followed like robots. We knew exactly where we were going. We just didn't know what was going to happen when we got there. We followed Mr. Lee down the hidden stairs, through the long hallway, and right to the door of his secret studio. The first thing I saw was the alien robot. He was sitting at a table, eating something green and lumpy. The next second, everything went dark.

"Hey, Morgan, wake up! Wake up!" Lewis was shaking me. It took me a few seconds to remember where I was, and then I sat up fast. The room seemed bright—too bright—but then my eyes adjusted.

"You fainted," said Lewis. He was behind me. I scanned the room. The alien robot was still sitting down, but something was different. Now he was watching me, staring at me. I looked around. Who had the remote? Who was making him move? I pressed back against Lewis.

Mr. Lee shoved a paper cup of water in front of me. "Don't worry about him. Drink."

"That's Thoam," said Lewis. "He's not a robot. He's

actually really nice." I knew that tone of voice. Lewis was showing off—like he knew something I didn't. I don't know why that helped, but it did. I stood up.

Mr. Lee pointed to the table with the alien robot. "How about we sit down."

Lewis patted me on the shoulder. "He's from outer space, but he's not dangerous. In fact, he's saving our world."

I turned around. "How do you know all this? How long was I out?"

Lewis held up his hands. "That's all I know. Maybe four minutes."

"Three minutes and twelve seconds," said a voice. It was a new voice, a voice I'd never heard before. I turned back toward the table. The alien robot lifted its arm and waved at me.

At first I was nervous to sit next to him, but the more he talked, the better I liked him. Thoam said he'd programmed his voice to be pleasing to humans, and he'd done an excellent job.

"I have a lot to tell you," said Thoam. "The—"

Suddenly Mr. Lee cut him off. "Did you write your plankton paragraph?"

Lewis and I both nodded.

I thought Mr. Lee might want us to go home and get them, but he scowled and said, "We don't have time for that."

Mr. Lee could learn a lesson about niceness from Thoam. It's not a good sign when someone starts to like a scary-looking alien better than a real human.

Three Things I Learned About Thoam

1) He was a real alien.
2) He wouldn't eat or hurt us!
3) He was here to save our world.
4) He could remember something forever, just by looking at it or hearing it once.

"It's time for a history lesson," said Thoam.

I'm not a big fan of history, but if learning about history was going to save the world, I'd pay attention. What Thoam told us was hard to believe, but if a real, live alien is telling you stuff, you should probably believe it.

The New History of the World
by Thoam

BACK IN THE AGE OF THE DINOSAURS, AN ALIEN FORCE WAS MAPPING THE UNIVERSE, LOOKING FOR PLANETS THAT PRODUCED PLANKTON, THEIR MAIN FOOD SOURCE.

Lewis and I both nodded. We knew about plankton, but we didn't know aliens would eat it. Was that what Thoam had been eating?

Thoam looked at me to be sure I was listening, then continued.

"The aliens found thousands and thousands of planets that had plankton, and your Earth was one of them. Beacons were set up on these planets, deep down underground. When the plankton reached a high level, sensors in the ocean would send a signal to the beacons, and they would rise to signal my planet that it was time to come and harvest the plankton."

I put my hand up. "Is a beacon kind of like that thing in the Thanksgiving turkey that pops up when it's cooked?"

Thoam looked confused, but Mr. Lee nodded. "Yes, somewhat. No more questions!"

POP ← THE EARTH IS READY TO BE EATEN.

Mrs. Shipley says that questions are a valuable part of learning, but I didn't say that to Mr. Lee. It was probably better just to listen.

Thoam was moving his arms around now. I figured that meant this part was important. I sat forward. "There are forty-six beacons implanted in your Earth, in oceans, in lakes, and on land. When all the beacons 'pop up,' the aliens will come."

Thoam looked right at me when he said *pop up*, so I smiled.

"I'm part of a rebel group who do not believe in harvesting plankton from planets with intelligent life. I came here in 1943 after the first beacon popped up, and I've been here ever since. I have been working with Mr. Lee since 1999. We were introduced through the EWWA program—Earthlings Working with Aliens. Mr. Lee is an expert robot builder and together we are trying to re-program the beacons so they go back underground. It's how I can save your Earth."

"Can't we just give them the plankton?" asked Lewis.

He was ignoring Mr. Lee's no-question rule, but Mr. Lee didn't say anything.

Thoam shook his head. "If your planet loses its plankton, the seas will die, and then your planet will die too."

I already knew that from my paragraph, but I didn't brag. Instead, I had more questions.

"Do the aliens want to eat us?"

Thoam shook his head.

"Are they going to fight us?"

He shook it again.

"Do all the beacons have to pop up for the aliens to come?"

He nodded.

I had more questions, but Lewis interrupted me. "What does the Sasquatch have to do with this? And why is it so stinky?"

Mr. Lee looked frustrated, though he didn't say anything.

Thoam continued. "All the beacons on Earth are now guarded by robots. The robots are very advanced, and they were created to fit into the landscape. They have one job—to protect the beacons. They stay near the beacons at all times. They work on their own, but if we need to, we can re-program them to work manually with a special remote. The robot in this area is disguised as a Sasquatch, and Mr. Lee added the special stink as a bonus to keep people away. It's called STINK 309."

When he said that last part, Mr. Lee looked right at me and narrowed his eyes.

We were in big trouble.

"Mr. Lee, we took your Sasquatch!" Lewis and I both said it at the exact same time.

Mr. Lee held up his hand. "I know all about it."

He pointed to a TV screen and suddenly there we were, Lewis and I making the Sasquatch lift up a giant log, me trying to take a photo, and Betty riding like a Sasquatch baby. The whole thing was on video.

Mr. Lee wagged his finger.

Lewis and I both looked down at the table.

"I don't know," said Thoam. "It seems like fun. Look at her. She's so happy."

I snuck a look at the video, and he was right. Betty was laughing. I hadn't noticed that when it was happening.

"Poor Thoam," said Mr. Lee. "He's always stuck in here with me. He never gets out and has a good time. An alien can't just walk around town like you and I."

I looked up at Thoam. "You'd like to get out and do stuff? With humans? Any humans? Even *girl* humans?"

Mr. Lee and Thoam were confused, but Lewis wasn't. He knew exactly what I was thinking.

Betty

I explained what Betty wanted, and then I held my breath. It was going to be a *no*. I just knew it.

"OK," said Thoam. "I'll dance with her."

It took a while, but after about fifteen minutes, Mr. Lee agreed to it too. That, all by itself, was kind of mind-blowing. Who knew Mr. Lee had a heart?

The plan was simple. Thoam would dance with Betty, and I would pretend to be controlling him with a remote. Betty would never and could never know that he was real.

Monday At School

I couldn't wait for the day to be over, but some good things happened. One of them was a huge surprise. Mrs. Shipley wore a Sasquatch shirt!

I guess Mrs. Shipley was OK, but it didn't change my mind about her reading tests. They were still the worst.

Lewis brought in a plaster cast of the Sasquatch footprint to show everyone. His parents had made a bunch of them to sell at the motel. Marcus Wolver asked to go to the bathroom as soon as Lewis took it out of his backpack. I don't know what he was doing in there, but he was gone a long time.

STUPID SASQUATCH!

PLAYING WITH THE TOILET PAPER

You wouldn't think an alien would be nervous to meet my sister, but Thoam was. I told him not to worry, but I don't think my pep talk helped. He spent a lot more time than I would have patting his shirt down so it looked just right.

But he was amazing. It took him only five seconds to learn the cha-cha. One look at the instructions and he was an expert. I couldn't wait.

THOAM DRESSED UP FOR THE DANCE

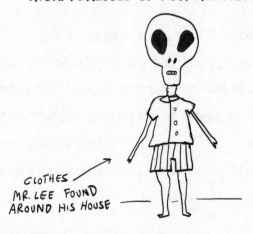

CLOTHES MR. LEE FOUND AROUND HIS HOUSE

While Lewis waited with Thoam at the motel, I went to get Betty. Earlier Mr. Lee had helped us get rid of Lewis's parents and Red for the night. He'd put a certificate for a free dinner for four through their door. Lewis's mom was surprised when Lewis said he couldn't go because he had to do homework. Sage was suspicious, so I had to come over after school and make up a whole story about the fake assignment that was due the next day. It worked, but the bad part was that she wanted to see our progress when she got back from dinner. We had to do fake homework! Neither of us was happy about that.

Since Mom was thinking that Betty and I were now buddies, she was happy and winked at me when Betty said she was coming with me to Lewis's house. I don't know what she thought we were going to be doing, but she didn't ask. The whole way over in the car, Betty kept poking me and whispering things like, "I hope you know what you're doing. That thing better not step on my feet." It made me wish for trouble.

I SHOULD TELL THOAM TO KICK HER, JUST ONCE.

Betty's Promise

As soon as Mom dropped us off, Betty raced toward the back of the motel. I just barely caught her arm before she got there. She turned and was about to swat me, but she changed her mind.

"WHAT?"

"You have to promise to be nice to the robot. Not to say nasty things about the way it looks or feels. It's very advanced, and Mr. Lee said if you do things like that, it'll stop working."

Betty looked at me like I was crazy. I stared back at her, trying to make my eyes seem menacing.

She snorted. "Fine, whatever. Just stop with the creepy eyes."

It was a victory.

KEEPING HER PROMISE AND NOT SAYING ANYTHING

The Dance

Betty was shocked when she saw Thoam. She just stood there staring with her mouth open, but she kept her promise and didn't say anything. Then, after a minute, she walked up and stood right in front of him. She turned to me. "It's bigger than you said it would be, but if you can make it dance, I'll work with it."

Lewis was standing next to me. He raised his eyebrows.

"I know," I whispered. "She's evil."

Lewis had one job. He reached over, pushed PLAY, and the music started. Betty spun around and looked at us. The music was a surprise, but it wasn't for her—it was for Thoam. A minute later they were dancing. My sister was dancing with an alien. If they hadn't been so good, I would have been rolling on the floor laughing.

My job was easy. All I had to do was fiddle with the fake remote. After about ten minutes, Betty yelled for us to stop. Thoam froze, and I went running over to see what was wrong.

Betty's face was red, but she was smiling. She grabbed me and gave me a surprise hug. Instead of saying something mean, I think I heard her say *Thank you*, but it was kind of faint, so I can't be sure. I was shocked. We both stood there for a moment, and then she punched me in the arm and pointed to my chair.

"Get back there. Let's dance."

When I got back, Lewis quizzed me.

"What was that about?"

I pointed at Thoam. "I think she likes him."

Lewis smiled. "Maybe he likes her too."

What Happened Next

A lot of things happened after that. Some were good for me, some were good for Lewis, some were good for Betty, and some were good for Thoam.

What Was Good for Me

Betty was definitely nicer to me—not so nice that anyone else would notice, but I did. When she got me in a headlock, she didn't squeeze as hard. It was a small thing, but I appreciated it.

What Was Good for Lewis

He's staying in Twin Rivers and doesn't have to move. The motel business is doing really great now because of the Sasquatch footprint, and his mom promised they weren't going to go anywhere for at least a year. That was good news, because when a mom says something, it's usually true.

What Was Almost Good For Betty

Betty didn't get to be partners with Dylan. Some girl in the eighth grade won, and Betty came in second. I thought she'd be upset, but she wasn't. She was more excited that Dylan now knows her name, and when she passes him at school, he mostly always says hi. She says all her friends are so jealous.

What Was Good For Thoam

Thoam loved dancing with Betty. Every time we see him, he talks about it. I told Mr. Lee that he's got to find a way for Thoam to get out more. Dancing with my crazy sister can't be the highlight of Thoam's life. I thought Mr. Lee would do his usual thing—hold up his hand and tell me to be quiet—but he didn't.

Instead he said, "You're right. He can go out when Goshzilla gets here."

GOSHZILLA? GIANT LIZARD OF DOOM?

SUPER SASQUATCH SHOWDOWN

BONUS MATERIALS

GOFISH

CHARISE MERICLE HARPER

What was your inspiration for the Sasquatch and Aliens series?
When I was young, my parents had a friend who owned a motel near Hope in British Columbia. It was called the Sasquatch Inn. Behind the inn were a series of caves that were something of a tourist attraction at the time. You had to climb down old ladders, scramble over rocks, and keep your flashlight sweeping around you for safety. It was thrilling. And then when you got to the very back of the cave everyone would turn off their flashlights and scream. I was terrified and I loved it.

Have you ever had any alien or Sasquatch encounters?
No, but I always thought it would be cool to see a UFO. I still look for them in the sky at night—because you never know.

What is your favorite moment in the book and why?
My favorite moments are Morgan's inner dialogues. In real life you never know what other people are thinking, so it's nice to have this ability to *go behind the scenes* in a book.

What did you want to be when you grew up?
I had no idea. Maybe an artist?

When did you realize you wanted to be a writer?
Uh . . . Is that what I am? I don't really consider myself a writer.
I'm more comfortable with the term story wrangler.

What's your most embarrassing childhood memory?
There are too many to write about. Here's an early one. When
a boy in third grade kissed my sweater in front of the whole
class. That was not cool.

What's your favorite childhood memory?
Playing with my younger brother, and dancing with my mom
and brother while we did the dishes after dinner.

As a young person, who did you look up to most?
Teachers. I was a very respectful student.

What was your favorite thing about school?
Making covers for the projects we had to write. I loved art.

**What were your hobbies as a kid? What are your
hobbies now?**
Let's see—I had a rock collection for a while, but that got
boring. I loved drawing, reading, and looking for the fun in
any situation. My hobbies are the same except for the rock
collection.

Did you play sports as a kid?
No, I did not play sports.

**What was your first job, and what was your "worst"
job?**
My first job was babysitting and my worst job was cleaning
bathrooms.

What book is on your nightstand now?
Roller Girl by Victoria Jamieson.

How did you celebrate publishing your first book?
We went out to dinner with my daughter, who was also new at the time. To be honest, I was more excited about her than the book.

Where do you write your books?
I write at my kitchen table, in my studio, and at the library. I use a laptop.

What challenges do you face in the writing process, and how do you overcome them?
I have a schedule and I try to keep to it. For me, routine is the ticket.

Who is your favorite fictional character?
I like all of Jane Austen's characters.

What was your favorite book when you were a kid? Do you have a favorite book now?
I was a big fan of Richard Scarry books. I like looking at all the characters and imagining what they were doing.

If you could travel in time, where would you go and what would you do?
I'd go back in time to meet my mom when she was twenty. I'd love to know her then.

What's the best advice you have ever received about writing?
Just do it.

What advice do you wish someone had given you when you were younger?
Find what you like—think creatively. Can you find a way to support yourself? Don't worry what everyone else thinks. Try.

Do you ever get writer's block? What do you do to get back on track?
I do get stymied. When that happens, I leave what I'm doing and try something else. With time off, my brain quietly works out the problem. It might take days or weeks, but it always happens. I just have to be patient. That's the hard part.

What do you want readers to remember about your books?
That they had fun reading them.

If you were a superhero, what would your superpower be?
Writing as fast as people can read.

Do you have any strange or funny habits? Did you when you were a kid?
I talk to myself—probably more than I should.

What do you consider to be your greatest accomplishment?
Being a mom.

What would your readers be most surprised to learn about you?
That I can't walk by a shoe store without going in.

Don't miss where the
Sasquatch and alien fun began!

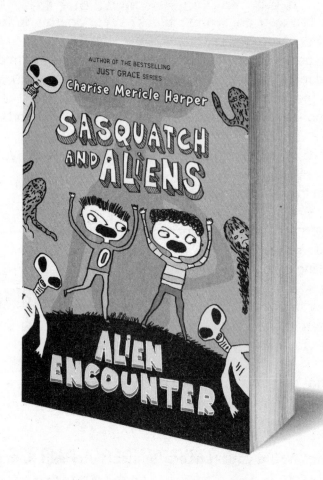

Keep reading for an excerpt.

An Acrostic Poem About Lewis

LIVES IN A MOTEL.

EATS STRANGE FOODS.

WILL DO ALMOST ANYTHING.

IS NEW IN TOWN.

SLEEPS UNDER A PAIR OF RIPPED UNDERPANTS.

Why I Met Lewis

I met Lewis because of underpants. This is not a normal way to meet someone. When weird things happen, they are usually a surprise.

KINDS OF UNDERPANTS

PLAIN
BOXERS

BOXERS
WITH
PATTERN

PLAIN
WHITE
UNDERPANTS

LEWIS'S
KIND

UNDERPANTS
WITH A
PATTERN

The Woods

Lewis and I met in the woods. I don't know what he was doing, but I was there looking for a stick. It was for my new invention—the triple slingshot. Slingshots are easy to make. The only hard part is finding the right stick, and if you need lots of sticks to choose from, the woods are the perfect place to look. They're filled with sticks. If I'd been looking for a regular stick, I probably would have been done in about two seconds, but I wasn't. Special sticks take a lot longer to find.

THE SPECIAL STICK

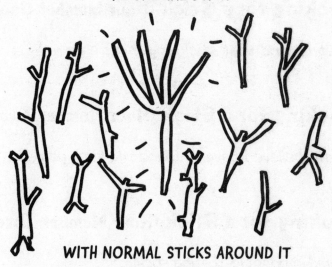

WITH NORMAL STICKS AROUND IT

An Acrostic About What I Will Make with the Perfect Stick

SUPER SLINGSHOT.

TRIPLE FIRING POWER.

IT NEVER MISSES.

CAN HIT THREE TARGETS AT ONCE.

KING OF THE SLINGSHOTS.

Looking for a Stick (Hour Number One)

I bet I'll find that stick any minute now.

Looking for a Stick (Hour Number Two)

I can't believe I haven't found the stick yet.

Looking for a Stick (Hour Number Three)

Stupid impossible-to-find stick!

It's not easy to think good thoughts when you've been disappointed for almost 10,800 seconds in a row. That's probably why I suddenly remembered Dad's saying.

DAD LOOKING HAPPY WHILE HE SAYS SOMETHING THAT MAKES THE PERSON HE IS TALKING TO SAD.

JUST BECAUSE YOU WANT SOMETHING DOESN'T MEAN YOU'RE GOING TO GET IT.

Sometimes it's hard to tell if the stuff Dad says is true or not. He tells jokes without laughing, and says real things while smiling. He's a confusing guy. Even though I didn't want to believe him, my brain was starting to think that maybe his saying was true. Maybe I wouldn't find my stick or, worse, maybe it didn't even exist.

THINGS THAT DO NOT EXIST

TIME MACHINES

SUPERPOWERS

MY STICK

The One Thing You Should Be Scared of if You Hear It in the Woods

SCREAMING!

If you are in the woods and you hear screaming, your first thought should be **DANGER!**

A good idea for a second thought would be **BEAR ATTACK!**

BAD IDEAS FOR A SECOND THOUGHT

NAP TIME	TOILET TIME	DANCE TIME
TACO TIME	JUMPING JACK TIME	SINGING TIME

I don't know if Twin Rivers has ever had a real bear attack, but last year we had an almost bear attack. My across-the-street neighbor Mrs. Lee saw a bear in her backyard. He could have eaten her, except she was inside getting some iced tea to drink with her lunch.

She said, "Iced tea saved my life!"

Our whole town knew about it because she got to be on TV, and every time the camera did a close-up, she said the exact same thing. "Iced tea saved my life!" She probably said it more than twenty times.

Mrs. Lee said she was filling her glass with iced tea when she looked out her window and saw a big, furry thing sitting at her picnic table. It was a bear, and he was eating her lunch. He ate her tuna sandwich, her strawberries, and even her broccoli salad (he must have been really hungry to eat that).

She took a ton of pictures. One of them even got in the paper. It was a picture of the bear at the table with the sandwich in his paws. He was sitting up and looked just like a person, except he was furry, had huge claws and teeth, and could totally kill you.

BEAR

Everyone at school was super excited about the bear, until Marcus Wolver kind of ruined it. He made up a fake rumor. Most people didn't believe him, but a few did, and that was annoying because now instead of everyone being excited, some people were grumpy about the Lees.

The Thing That Is Wrong with Marcus

Marcus is a nincompoop.

Normally, I wouldn't pick a dumb word like that, but Mom said I'm not even allowed to think about the other word I wanted to use. She's pretty bossy about stuff like that. She says old-fashioned words are more polite, but that's probably just because no one knows what they mean.

YOUNG PERSON

I made up an acrostic to help describe Marcus and the word *nincompoop*—I think it helps.

M OSTLY IS ANNOYING.

A LWAYS TRIES TO STEAL JUICE BOXES AT LUNCHTIME.

R EALLY THINKS HE IS AWESOME.

C AN ARGUE ABOUT ANYTHING.

U H . . . WHAT HE SAYS WHENEVER A TEACHER ASKS HIM A QUESTION.

S PITS WHILE HE TALKS . . . ON PURPOSE!

Marcus was wrong about the Lees for a lot of reasons, but the main reason he was wrong was that he didn't know them. This is important because if he knew them, he'd know that the Lees are not costume-loving people, and people who do not like costumes do not run around in bear suits.

I know this because the Lees are my neighbors, and even if you don't want to, you learn stuff about people when they live right across the street from you.